The Mystery
of the
Disappearing Cat

The Second Adventure of
the Five Find-Outers and
Buster their Dog

Granada Publishing Limited
Published in 1966 by Dragon Books
3 Upper James Street, London W1R 4BP
Reprinted 1967, 1968, 1969, 1970, 1971

First published by Methuen & Co Ltd 1944
Copyright © Enid Blyton 1944
Made and printed in Great Britain by
C. Nicholls & Company Ltd
The Philips Park Press, Manchester
Set in Intertype Times

The Mystery of the Disappearing Cat

Enid Blyton

Cover illustration by Peter Archer
Text illustrations by Mary Gernat

Dragon

Dark Queen disappeared into the bushes

The Big Boy Next Door

Bets was feeling very excited. Her big brother Pip was coming home from school that day for the long summer holidays. She had been without him for three months, and had felt very lonely. Now she would have him again.

"And Larry and Daisy will be home tomorrow!" she said to her mother. "Oh, Mummy! it will be fun to have so many children to play with again."

Larry and Daisy were Pip's friends. They were older than Bets, but they let her play with them. In the Easter holidays the four of them, with another boy and his dog, had had a great adventure finding out who had burnt down a cottage.

"We were the Five Find-Outers," said Bets, remembering everything. "We found out the whole mystery, Mummy, didn't we? Oh, I do wish we could solve another mystery these holidays too!"

Her mother laughed. "Oh, it was just a bit of luck that you solved the mystery of the burnt cottage," she said. "There won't be any more mysteries, so don't expect any, Bets. Now hurry up and get ready. It's time to meet Pip."

Pip was most excited to be home again. When he got back with Bets he tore round the garden, looking at everything. It seemed to him as if he had been away for years.

His little sister tore round with him, chattering at the top of her voice all the time. She adored Pip, but he didn't take very much notice of her. To him she was only just a little girl, still a baby, who liked her dolls, and cried when she fell down.

"Larry and Daisy are coming back tomorrow," she panted, as she rushed round after Pip. "Oh, Pip! do you think we can be the Find-Outers again?"

"Only if there is something to find out, silly," said Pip. "Oh! I forgot to tell you, Fatty is coming for the holidays too. His parents liked Peterswood so much when they stayed here at Easter, that they have bought a little house, and Fatty will be here for the hols."

"Oh, *good*!" said Bets happily. "I like Fatty. He's kind to me. We shall really be the Five Find-Outers again then; and oh, Pip! I suppose Buster is coming, isn't he?"

"Of course," said Pip. Buster was Fatty's little black Scottie dog, loved by all the children. "It will be nice to see old Buster again."

"How do you know about Fatty coming?" asked Bets, still trotting round after Pip.

"He wrote to me," said Pip. "Wait a minute – I've got the letter here. He sent a message to you in it."

The boy felt in his pockets and took out a crumpled letter. Bets took it from him eagerly. It was very short, written in extremely neat handwriting.

"DEAR PIP, – Just to say my parents have bought White House, not far from you, so I'll be seeing you in the summer hols. Hope we have another mystery to solve. It would be fun to be the Five Find-Outers and Dog again. Give my love to little Bets. I'll pop down and see you as soon as I get back. – Yours,
FREDERICK ALGERNON TROTTEVILLE."

"Why doesn't he sign himself Fatty?" asked Bets. "I think Frederick Algernon Trotteville sounds so silly."

"Well, Fatty *is* silly sometimes," said Pip. "I hope he won't come back full of himself. Do you remember how he kept boasting about his marvellous bruises last hols, when he fell off that hayrick?"

"Well, they *were* most awfully good bruises," said Bets, remembering. "They did turn a wonderful colour. I wish my bruises went like that."

Larry and Daisy came back the next day about three

o'clock. After tea they raced off to see Pip and Bets. It was lovely to be all together again. Bets felt a little left-out after a bit, because she was the only one who did not go to boarding-school, and did not understand some of the things the others said.

"I wish I wasn't only eight years old," she thought for about the thousandth time. "Larry's thirteen, and the others are twelve – ages older than me. I shall never catch them up."

Just as they were all exchanging their news, and laughing and chattering gaily, there came the scampering of feet up the drive, and a small black Scottie dog hurled himself into the middle of them, yapping excitedly.

"It's Buster! Oh, Buster, you're back again!" cried Daisy in delight. "Good old Buster!"

"Dear old Buster! You're fatter!"

"Hallo, Buster-dog! Glad to see you, old fellow!"

"Darling Buster! I've missed you so!"

They were all so engaged in making a fuss of the excited little dog that they didn't see Fatty, Buster's master, walking up to them. Bets saw him first. She jumped to her feet with a squeal, and rushed to Fatty. She flung her arms round him and hugged him. Fatty was pleased. He liked little Bets. He gave her a hug back.

The others grinned at him. "Hallo, Fatty!" said Larry. "Had a good term?"

"I was top of my form," said Fatty, not looking very modest about it.

"He's the same old Fatty," said Pip with a grin. "Top of this, that, and the other – full of brains as usual – best boy in the school!"

"Shut up," said Fatty, giving Pip a friendly punch. "I suppose *you* were bottom of *your* form!"

It was lovely to lie on the grass, play with Buster, and think of the eight or nine long sunny weeks ahead. No lessons. No rules. No being kept in or writing out lines. The summer holidays were really the nicest of all.

"Any news, Bets?" asked Fatty. "Any mysteries turned up? Any problems to solve? We're still the Five Find-Outers and Dog, don't forget!"

"I know," said Bets happily. "But there isn't any mystery at present, Fatty. I haven't even seen old Clear-Orf for weeks."

Clear-Orf was the burly village Policeman, Mr. Goon. The children always called him Clear-Orf, because that was what he said whenever he saw them. He didn't like children, and they didn't like him.

"Bets just hasn't any news at all," said Pip. "Nothing at all seems to have happened in Peterswood since we left to go to school."

Bets suddenly remembered something. "Oh, I've just remembered," she said. "Somebody has come to live next door."

The house next door had been empty for a year or two. The other children looked at Bets. "Any children there?" asked Pip.

"No," said Bets. "At least, I don't think so. I've seen a big boy there, but I think he works in the garden. I hear him whistling sometimes. He whistles awfully nicely. Oh, and there are lots of cats there – very funny cats."

"*Cats?* What sort of cats?" said Pip in surprise, and Buster pricked up his ears and growled at the mention of cats.

"They've got dark-brown faces and tails and legs," said Bets, "and cream-coloured fur. I saw the girl who looks after them carrying one once. It looked very queer."

"She means Siamese cats," said Larry. "Have they got bright blue eyes, Bets?"

"I don't know," said Bets. "I wasn't near enough to see. Anyway, cats have green eyes, not blue, Larry."

"Siamese cats have bright blue ones," said Fatty. "I know, because my aunt once had one – a beauty, called Patabang. They are valuable cats."

"I'd like to go in next door and see them some day,"

said Daisy, thinking that a cat with bright blue eyes, dark-brown face, legs, and tail, and cream-coloured fur sounded very lovely. "Who's the owner, Bets?"

"Somebody called Lady Candling," said Bets. "I've never seen her. She is away a lot, I think."

The children lay on their backs talking. Buster went from one to another, licking their faces and making them squeal and push him away.

Then there came the sound of a cheerful whistling just over the wall. It was a fine whistle, clear and melodious.

"That's the big boy next door I told you about," said Bets. "Doesn't he whistle nicely?"

Larry got up and went to the wall. He hopped up on a big flower-pot and looked over the wall. He saw a boy there, about fifteen, a big lad with a round red face, startlingly blue eyes that looked rather surprised, and a big mouth full of very white teeth. The lad was hoeing the bed below the wall.

He looked up when he saw someone peeping over. He grinned, showing all his white teeth.

"Hallo," said Larry. "Are you the gardener next door?"

"Lawks! no," said the boy, grinning even more widely. "I'm just the boy – the gardener's boy, I'm called. Mr. Tupping is the gardener – him with the hooky nose and bad temper."

Larry didn't think that Mr. Tupping sounded very nice. He glanced up the garden, but Mr. Tupping and his hooky nose were not in sight.

"Could we come over and see the cats one day?" asked Larry. "It's Siamese cats, isn't it, that Lady Candling has?"

"Yes. Lovely creatures they are," said the boy. "Well, you'd better come when Mr. Tupping is out. He reckons that the whole place is his, cats and all, the way he behaves. Come in tomorrow afternoon. He'll be out then. You can get over this wall. The kennel-girl will be here – Miss Harmer her name is. She won't mind you seeing the cats."

"Righto!" said Larry, pleased. "We'll be over here to-morrow afternoon. I say – what's your name?"

But before the boy could answer him, an angry voice sounded from not far off.

"Luke! Luke! Where have you got to? Didn't I tell you to clear away that rubbish? Drat the boy, he's no use at all."

Luke raised startled blue eyes to Larry, and put his hoe over his shoulder. He looked scared.

"That's him," he said in a whisper. "That's Mr. Tupping. I'll be going now. You come on over tomorrow."

He went up the path. Larry slipped back to the others. "He's the garden boy," he said. "His name's Luke. He looks nice, but a bit simple. I shouldn't think he could say boo to a goose."

Bets felt certain she couldn't either, because geese were big and hissy. "Are we to see the cats tomorrow?" she asked. "I heard you saying something about them."

"Yes. Tomorrow afternoon, when Mr. Tupping the gardener is out," said Larry. "We'll hop over the wall. Better not take old Buster though – you know what he is with cats!"

Buster growled when he heard the word. Cats! What did the children want to go and see cats for? Silly useless animals, with paws full of nasty pins and needles! Cats were only good for one thing, and that was – to chase!

Horrid Mr. Tupping!

The next afternoon Larry went to the wall and whistled for Luke.

The boy came along after a while, smiling and showing

10

his white teeth. "It's safe to come," he said. "Mr. Tupping is out."

Soon all the children were over the wall. Fatty helped Bets. Buster was left behind and was most annoyed about it. He barked angrily, and stood up on his hind legs, pawing the wall desperately.

"Poor Buster," said Bets, sorry for him. "Never mind, Buster – we'll soon be back."

"No dogs allowed in here," said Luke. "Because of the cats, you know. They're prize cats. Won no end of money, so the kennel-girl says."

"Do you live here?" asked Larry, as they all walked up the path towards some big greenhouses.

"No. I live with my stepfather," said Luke. "My mother's dead. I got no brothers or sisters. This is my first job. My name's Luke Brown, and I'm fifteen."

"Oh," said Larry. "I'm Laurence Daykin, and I'm thirteen. This is Margaret, my sister. She's twelve. We call her Daisy. This is Frederick Algernon Trotteville. He's twelve too, and he's called Fatty."

"I'd rather be called Frederick, thanks," said Fatty, in a cross voice. "There's no reason for me to be called Fatty by every Tom, Dick, and Harry! "

"You aren't Tom, Dick, or Harry, you're called Luke, aren't you?" said Bets to Luke. He grinned.

"I'll call you Frederick if you like," he said to Fatty. "By rights I should call you Master Frederick, but I guess you don't want me to."

"I'm Elizabeth Hilton, and I'm eight, and I'm called Bets," said Bets, afraid that Larry was going to leave her out. "And this is Philip, my brother. He's twelve and he's called Pip."

They told Luke where they lived, and he told them where he lived – in a tumbledown cottage by the river. By this time they had left the greenhouses behind and were going through a beautiful rose-garden. Beyond it rose a green-painted building.

"That's the cat-house," said Luke. "And there's Miss Harmer."

A plump young woman, dressed in corduroy coat and breeches, was near the cat-house. She looked surprised to see the five children.

"Hallo," she said, "where have *you* come from?"

"We came over the wall," said Larry. "We wanted to see the cats. They're not ordinary ones, are they?"

"Oh no," said Miss Harmer. She was a big, strapping girl of about twenty. "There they are – do you like them?"

The children gazed into the big cage-like building. There were quite a number of cats there, all with the same striking colouring – dark-brown and cream, with brilliant blue eyes. They stared at the children, and miaowed in most peculiar voices.

"They're lovely," said Daisy, at once.

"I think they look queer," said Pip.

"Are they really cats? They look a bit like monkeys," said Bets. The others laughed.

"You wouldn't think they were monkeys once you felt their sharp claws!" said Miss Harmer, with a laugh. "All these cats are prize ones – they have been to shows and won a lot of money."

"Which one has won the most money?" said Bets.

"This one over here," said Miss Harmer, and she led the way to a smaller cage, like a very large kennel on legs. "Well, Dark Queen? Aren't you a beauty? Here are some visitors to tell you how lovely you are!"

The big Siamese cat in the large, airy cage rubbed her head against the wire-netting, mewing loudly. The kennel-girl scratched her gently on the head.

"Dark Queen is our very, very special cat," she said. "She has just won a prize of a hundred pounds. She is worth much more than that."

Dark Queen stood up, and her dark-brown tail rose in the air, swaying gently to and fro. Bets noticed something.

"She's got a few creamy hairs in the middle of her dark tail," she said to Miss Harmer.

"Yes," said the kennel-girl. "She was bitten by one of the others there, and the hairs grew cream instead of brown. But they will turn brown later. What do you think of her?"

"Well – she seems just exactly like all the others," said Daisy. "I mean – they are exactly alike, aren't they?"

"Yes, they are," said Miss Harmer. "They have exactly the same colouring, you see. But I can always tell the difference, even when they are all mixed up together."

"Fancy being worth more than a hundred pounds!" said Fatty, staring at Dark Queen, who stared back with unwinking blue eyes.

"Could you get Dark Queen out?" asked Daisy, who was longing to hold the beautiful cat. "Is she tame?"

"Oh *yes*," said Miss Harmer. "They are all tame. We only keep them in cages because they are so valuable. We couldn't let them roam free in case someone stole them."

She took a key from a nail, and unlocked the cage-door. She lifted Dark Queen out, and held her. The beautiful cat rubbed against her, purring in a deep voice. Daisy stroked her, and to her delight the cat jumped into her arms.

"Oh, isn't she friendly?" said Daisy joyfully.

Then there came a great disturbance! Buster suddenly rushed along the path and flung himself on Fatty, barking joyfully. Dark Queen leapt straight out of Daisy's arms, and disappeared into the bushes. Buster, surprised, stared for a moment, and then, with a loud and joyful yelp, plunged after her. There was a terrific scrimmage.

Miss Harmer squealed. Luke's mouth fell open and he looked frightened. All the cats set up a miaowing. Fatty called fiercely:

"Buster! Come here, sir! BUSTER! Do you hear me? COME HERE, SIR!"

But no amount of calling could get Buster away if there

was a cat to chase. Miss Harmer ran in despair to the bushes. Only Buster was there, his nose bleeding from a scratch, his tongue hanging out, his eyes very bright and excited.

"Where's Dark Queen?" wailed Miss Harmer. "Oh, this is awful! Puss, puss, puss!"

Bets began to cry. She couldn't bear to think that Dark Queen had gone. She thought she heard a noise in some bushes right at the end of the path and she ran off to see, tears running down her fat cheeks.

Then there came another commotion. Someone walked up to the cages, came round them – and it was Mr. Tupping, the gardener! Luke stared at him in fright.

"What's all this?" shouted Mr. Tupping. "Who are you? What are you doing in my garden?"

"It isn't your garden," said Fatty boldly. "It's Lady Candling's, and she's a friend of my mother's."

It wasn't a bit of good telling Mr. Tupping that it wasn't his garden. He felt that it belonged to him. And here were children and a dog in *his* garden! He detested children, dogs, cats, and birds.

"You get out of here," he shouted in an angry voice. "Go on! Get out at once! Do you hear me? And if I catch you here again I'll box your ears and tell your fathers. Miss Harmer, what's the matter with *you*?"

"Dark Queen is gone!" wailed Miss Harmer, who seemed just as much afraid of Mr. Tupping as Luke.

"Serves you right if you lose your job," said Mr. Tupping. "What use are them cats, I'd like to know? Just rubbish, that's all they are. Good riddance if one *is* gone!"

"Shall we stay and help you to look for Dark Queen?" said Daisy to the Kennel-girl.

"You get out," said Mr. Tupping, and his big hooky nose got very red. His stone-coloured eyes glared at Daisy. He was an ugly, bad-tempered-looking fellow, with straw-coloured hair streaked with grey, and the children didn't like the look of him at all.

14

Tupping made a grab for Buster

They decided to go. Tupping looked as if he might hit them at any moment. They made their way to the wall. They saw that Bets was not with them, but they thought she must have run back and climbed over the wall in her fear of the surly gardener. Fatty called Buster.

"No; you leave that dog with me," said Tupping. "A good hiding will do him good. I'll give him one, then he won't come interfering in *my* garden again."

"Don't you dare to touch my dog! " cried Fatty at once. "He'll bite you."

Tupping made a grab for Buster and got him by the collar. He held him firmly by the back of the neck so that he couldn't even snap. He jerked him off his feet into the air, and then, carrying him by the back of the neck, marched off with him. Fatty was almost beside himself with anger.

He ran after the gardener and pulled at his arm. The man hit out at the boy, and Fatty gasped. Tupping threw the dog into a shed, shut the door, turned the key and put it into his pocket. Then he turned to Fatty with such an ugly look on his face that the boy turned and ran.

Soon all four were over the wall, lying on the grass, panting and angry. They had left poor frightened Luke behind, and poor scared Miss Harmer. They had left Bets behind too, though they didn't know it – and Buster was locked in the shed.

"Hateful man! " said Daisy, almost in tears.

"The beast! " said Fatty between his teeth. "Look at this bruise already showing on my arm. That's where he hit me."

"Poor old Buster," said Pip, hearing an anguished whine in the distance.

"Where's Bets?" said Larry, looking all round. "Bets, Bets! Where are you?"

There was no answer. Bets was still over the wall. "She must have gone indoors," said Pip. "I say, what are we

16

going to do about Buster? Fatty, we've got to rescue him, you know. We can't leave him there. I bet he *will* whip the poor little dog."

"Poor Buster," said Daisy. "And poor Dark Queen. Oh! I do hope she is found. I wonder how Buster got over the wall."

"He didn't," said Fatty. "He couldn't. He must have thought hard, run down the drive, and up the drive next door and into the garden to find us. You know what brains Buster has got. Oh, golly! how are we going to rescue him? How I hate that man Tupping! How awful for poor Luke to have to work under him! "

"I'll go and find Bets," said Pip. "She must have gone to hide or something – maybe she's scared."

He went into the house to find her, and soon came out looking puzzled. "She's not anywhere about," he said. "I've called and called. Wherever can she be? I suppose she *did* come back over the wall? She can't be in next door's garden still, can she?"

But she was. Poor little Bets was hiding there, scared stiff. What was she to do? She couldn't get over the wall by herself – and she didn't dare to run down the drive in case Mr. Tupping saw her!

Luke is a Good Friend

When Bets had run to the bushes to see if Dark Queen was there, she had found that it was only a big blackbird that had flown out as soon as she had got there. All the same, she went into the bushes and had a look round, calling, "Puss, puss, puss! "

Suddenly she saw two bright blue eyes looking down at her from the tree above. She jumped. Then she gave a cry of delight.

"Oh, it's you, Dark Queen! Oh, I'm so glad I've found you!"

She stood and thought. It was no good getting Dark Queen down until Buster was safely out of the garden. The lovely cat was much safer where she was. Bets looked up at Dark Queen and the cat began to purr. She liked the little girl.

Bets saw that the tree would be easy to climb. It wasn't long before she was up on the branch beside the cat, stroking her, and talking to her. Dark Queen simply loved it. She rubbed her dark brown head against the little girl, and purred very loudly.

And then Bets heard Mr. Tupping shouting, and she was frightened. Oh dear! the gardener must have come back. He wasn't out after all. She listened to the angry yelling, and trembled. She did not dare to join the others. She sat quietly by the cat and listened.

She could not hear exactly what happened, but after a while she realized that the others must have gone back over the wall and left her. She felt very forlorn and frightened. She was just about to slip down the tree to try and find Miss Harmer and tell her where Dark Queen was, when footsteps came along the path. The little girl peeped between the leaves of the tree and saw Mr. Tupping dragging poor Luke along by one of his big ears.

"I'll teach you to let children into my garden!" said Mr. Tupping, and he gave Luke such a slap that the boy let out a yell. "You're paid to do work, you are. You'll stay here and work two hours overtime for letting them children in!"

He gave Luke another blow, pulled his ear hard, then pushed him and sent him flying down the path. Bets was so sorry for Luke that tears ran down her cheeks, and she gave a little sob. Horrid Mr. Tupping!

Mr. Tupping went off down another path. Luke picked up a hoe, and was just setting off in the opposite direction when Bets called softly to him:

"Luke!"

Luke dropped his hoe with a clatter, and looked all round, startled. He could see no one. "Luke!" called Bets again. "I'm here, up the tree. And Dark Queen is with me."

Then Luke saw the little girl up the tree and the Siamese cat beside her. Bets slipped down and stood beside him.

"Help me over the wall, Luke," she said.

"Well, if Mr. Tupping sees me I'll lose my job, and my stepfather will belt me black and blue," said poor Luke, his big red face as scared as Bets' little one.

"Well, I don't want you to lose your job," said Bets. "I'll try and get over by myself."

But Luke would not let her do that. Scared as he was, he felt that he must help the little girl. He lifted Dark Queen down from the tree, and together the two of them walked softly up the path, keeping a sharp look-out for Mr. Tupping.

Luke slipped Dark Queen into her cage and shut the door. "Miss Harmer will be glad she's found," he whispered to Bets. "I'll tell her in a minute. Now, come on – sprint for the wall and I'll get you over."

They ran for the wall. Luke gave Bets a leg-up, and soon she was sitting on the top. "Buck up!" called Luke in a low voice. "Old Tupping is coming!"

Bets was so frightened that she jumped down at once, falling on hands and knees and grazing them. She rushed to the lawn, seeing the others there, and flung herself down beside them, trembling.

"Bets! Wherever have you been?" cried Pip.

"Were you left behind?" said Fatty. "Oh, look at your poor knees!"

"And my hands too," said Bets in a trembling voice, holding out bleeding hands. Fatty got out his hanky and wiped them. "How did you get over the wall by yourself?" he asked.

"I didn't. Luke helped me, though he was terribly, terribly afraid that Mr. Tupping would come along and catch

19

him. Then he would lose his job," said Bets.

"Jolly decent of him to help you, then," said Larry, and the others agreed.

"I like Luke," said Bets. "I think he's very, very nice. I do wish he hadn't got into trouble through letting us come over the wall and see the cats."

A distant whining came on the air again. Bets looked puzzled. She looked all round.

"Where's Buster?" she asked. She had not heard him being dragged away and locked up, though she had heard the noise of the commotion. The others told her. The little girl was indignant and upset.

"Oh, we *must* rescue him; we must, we must!" she cried. "Fatty, do, do go over the wall and get Buster!"

But Fatty didn't feel at all inclined to run the risk of meeting the surly Mr. Tupping again. Also he knew that the gardener had the key of Buster's shed in his pocket.

"If Lady Candling wasn't away I'd get my mother to ring her up and ask her to tell that fellow Tupping to set him free," said Fatty. He rolled up his sleeve again and looked at the big bruise on his arm, now turning red-purple. "If I showed my mother that, I bet she'd ring up a dozen Lady Candlings."

"It's going to be quite a good bruise," said Bets, knowing how proud Fatty always was of his bruises. "Oh dear, there's poor darling Buster howling again! Let's go to the wall and peep over. We might see Luke and get him to peep in at the shed window and say a kind word to Buster."

So they tiptoed cautiously to the wall and Larry carefully looked over. No one was about. Then there came the sound of someone whistling. It was Luke. Larry whistled too. The distant whistling stopped, then began again. It stopped, and Larry whistled the same tune.

Presently there came the sound of someone coming through the bushes and Luke's face appeared, full and red, like a round moon. "What's up?" he whispered. "I daren't stop. Mr. Tupping's still about."

"It's Buster," whispered Larry. "Can you peep in at the shed window and just say, 'Poor fellow,' or something like that to him?"

Luke nodded and disappeared. He went towards the shed, keeping a sharp look-out for the gardener. He saw him in the distance, taking off his coat to do a bit of work. He hung it on a nail outside one of the greenhouses. He caught sight of Luke and yelled at him.

"Now then, lazy! Have you finished that bed yet? I want you to come and tie up some tomatoes."

Luke shouted something back and went into the bushes nearby. He watched Mr. Tupping walk off to the kitchen-garden, unravelling some raffia as he went. The gardener disappeared through a green door let into the wall that ran round the kitchen-garden.

Then Luke did a very brave thing. He ran swiftly and quietly to Mr. Tupping's coat. He slipped his hand into the outer pocket, took the key of the little shed, and raced off with it. He unlocked the shed, and Buster rushed out. Luke tried to catch him in order to bundle him over the wall, but Buster escaped him and tore off down a path.

Luke locked the door quickly, ran back to the gardener's coat and slipped the key back into the pocket. Then he went to join Mr. Tupping in the kitchen-garden, hoping to goodness that Buster had had the sense to shoot off down the drive.

But Buster had lost his way. He suddenly appeared in the kitchen-garden and gave a yap of joy when he saw Luke. Mr. Tupping looked up at once.

"That dog!" he said in astonishment and anger. "Blessed if it isn't that dog again! How did he get out of the shed? Didn't I lock that door? And isn't the key in my pocket?"

"I saw you lock the door, sir," said Luke. "Perhaps it's a different dog."

Mr. Tupping waved his arms wildly and yelled at Buster. Buster gambolled into the kitchen-garden and ran right across a bed of carrots. Luke felt certain the little dog did it on purpose. Tupping went purple in the face.

"You get out!" he yelled, and threw a big stone at Buster. Buster yelped, and began to dig hard in the middle of the carrots, sending roots flying into the air.

Tupping went quite mad. He rushed over the carrot-bed, shouting, and Buster retired a good way off, and began to dig up some onions.

When a big stone came rather too near him Buster ran out of the green door in the kitchen-garden wall, and tore off down the nearest path. He soon found his way out of the garden, and went racing up the drive of Pip's house next door.

He flung himself joyfully on the surprised children. "Buster! Darling Buster! How did you get free? Oh, Buster, have you been hurt?"

Everyone spoke to Buster at once. He rolled over on his back and lay there, all his feet in the air, his tail thumping the ground and his pink tongue out.

"Good dog," said Fatty, patting his tummy. "I wish you could tell us how you got free!"

The children lay in wait for Luke that night as he went home. His time for knocking off was usually five, but that day Mr. Tupping kept him at work till seven as a punishment, and the boy, big and strong as he was, was tired out.

"Luke! How did Buster get free? Did you know he was free?" cried Pip. Luke nodded.

"Got the key out of old Tupping's coat meself and let the little dog out," he said. "Coo! you should have seen old Tupping's face when Buster came into the kitchen-garden. He nearly had a fit."

"Luke! Did you *really* let Buster out!" cried Fatty. He gave the big boy a thump on the back. "I say, thanks an awful lot! We were terribly upset about him. I guess you were scared to do it."

"Reckon I was," said Luke, scratching his head and remembering how scared he had felt. "But the little dog meant no harm and I guessed you'd all be worried about him."

"Oh, I do think you're nice, Luke," said little Bets, hanging on to his arm. "You got me safely over the wall, and you set Buster free. We'll all be your friends!"

"The likes of you can't be friends with the likes of me," said the big boy shyly, looking very pleased all the same.

"Well, we can," said Larry. "And what's more, in return for what you've done for us today, we promise to help *you* if ever you want help. See?"

"Don't reckon I'll want no help from kids like you," said big Luke in a friendly voice. "But thanks all the same. Don't you come over the wall any more now. You'll make me lose my job if you do."

"We won't," said Fatty. "And don't forget – if you're ever in real trouble, we'll help you, Luke!"

Miss Trimble Makes Trouble

Luke proved to be a most amusing friend to have. Certainly he was a bit "simple" and could hardly read or write, but he knew all kinds of things that the children didn't know.

He could make whistles out of hollow twigs, and he presented Bets with a wonderful collection. He showed her how to whistle little tunes on them, and she was thrilled.

Then he knew every bird in the countryside, where they nested, what their eggs were like, and the songs they sang. Soon the five children and Buster were going for walks with Luke, hanging on to his words, thinking that he was really marvellous.

"Funny he knows all that and yet can't read or write properly," said Pip. "He's terribly clever with his hands too – he can carve animals and birds out of bits of wood in no time. Look at this squirrel he did for me."

"He's doing a model of Dark Queen for me," said Bets proudly. "It's going to be exactly like her, even to the little ring of pale cream hairs in her dark-brown tail. Luke is going to paint the model for me, blue eyes and all."

Luke finished the wooden carving of Dark Queen, the Siamese cat, two days later. The children heard his now familiar whistle over the wall, and crowded there to see what he wanted. Luke handed over the cat-model.

It was really excellent. Even Fatty, who fancied himself very much at all kinds of art work, was very much impressed.

He handled the little model admiringly. "Fine, Luke," he said. "You've got the colouring marvellously too."

"How's old Tupping these days?" asked Pip.

"Awful," said Luke. "I wish I hadn't got to work for him. He's that bad-tempered. I'm always afraid of him complaining about me to my stepfather too. I'd get a good thrashing if he did. My stepfather doesn't like me."

The five children were sorry for Luke. He didn't seem to have much of a life. He was a kindly, generous fellow, always ready to do anything he could for them. He loved little Bets, and stuck up for her when Pip teased her, as he often did.

Buster adored Luke. "He's grateful to you for saving him from Tupping!" said Fatty, watching Buster trying to climb up Luke's legs, panting with delight.

"He's a nice little dog," said Luke. "I like dogs. Always did. I like them cats too. Beautiful things, aren't they?"

"We saw someone else in your garden today," said Larry. "A middle-aged lady, very thin, with a rather red nose, glasses that kept falling off, and a funny little bun of hair at the back of her neck. Who is she? That's not Lady Candling, is it?"

"Oh no," said Luke. "That's her companion, Miss Trimble. Miss *Tremble* I call her, to myself – she's that scared of old Tupping! She has to do the flowers for the house, you see; and if she goes out and picks them when Tupping is there, he follows her around like a dog ready to bite her, and says, 'If you pick any more of them roses, that'll spoil the tree!' 'If you take them poppies of mine they'll fall to bits – you shouldn't ought to pick them in the sun.' Things like that. The poor old thing trembles and shakes, and I feel right-down sorry for her."

"Everyone seems afraid of Tupping," said Daisy. "Horrid fellow. I hope he gets a punishment one day for being so hateful. But I bet he won't."

"Come and see my little garden, Luke," said Bets, pulling the big boy up the path. "It's got some lovely snapdragons out."

Luke went with her. It was a funny little garden, done by Bets herself. It had one old rose tree in it, a tiny gooseberry bush, some virginian stock, a few red snapdragons, and some Shirley poppies.

"Fine!" said Luke. "Did you have any gooseberries off that little bush?"

"Not one," said Bets sadly. "And Luke, I planted two strawberries last year – nice red ripe ones – and they didn't even grow up in strawberry plants. I was dreadfully disappointed. I did so want to pick strawberries of my own this year."

Luke laughed his loud, clear laugh. "Ho, ho, ho, ho! Strawberries don't grow from strawberries, Bets! They grow from runners – you know, long stems sent out from the plants. The runners send up little new plants here and there. I'll tell you what I'll do – I'll give you a few of our runners from next door. I'm cleaning up the beds now, and there'll be a lot of runners thrown away on the rubbish-heap. You can have some of those."

"Will it matter?" asked Bets doubtfully. "Would they really be rubbish?"

"Yes – all burnt up on the rubbish-heap!" said Luke. "It's Tupping's day off tomorrow. You come on over the wall and I'll show you how the runners grow, and give you some."

So the next day Pip helped Bets over the wall and Luke helped her down the other side. He took her to the strawberry-bed and showed her the new plants growing from the runners sent out from the old plants.

"It's very clever of the strawberries to grow new plants like that, isn't it?" said Bets. She saw a pile of pulled-up runners in Luke's barrow nearby. "Oh," she said, "are these the ones you're going to throw away? How many can I have?"

"You take six," said Luke, and he picked out six good runners, each with little healthy strawberry plants on them. He gave them to Bets.

"Who's that?" said Bets suddenly, as she saw someone coming towards them.

"It's Miss Trimble," said Luke. "You needn't be afraid of *her*. She won't hurt you."

Miss Trimble came up, smiled at Bets. Bets didn't like her very much, she was so thin and bony. She wore glasses without rims, pinched on to the sides of her nose. They kept falling off, and dangled on a little chain. Bets watched to see how many times they would fall off.

"Well, and who is *this* little girl?" said Miss Trimble, in a gay, bird-like voice, nodding at Bets. Her glasses at once fell off and she put them on again.

"I'm Bets from next door," said Bets.

"And what have you got there?" said Miss Trimble, looking at the strawberry plants in Bets' hands. "Some lovely treasure?"

"No," said Bets. "Just some strawberry runners."

Miss Trimble's glasses fell off again and she put them back.

"Be careful they don't run away from you!" she said, and laughed loudly at her own joke. Bets didn't think it was very funny; but she laughed too, out of politeness. Miss Trimble's glasses fell off again.

"Why don't they keep on?" asked Bets with interest. "Is your nose too thin to hold them on?"

"Oh, what a funny little girl!" said Miss Trimble, laughing again. "Well, good-bye my dear, I must away to my little jobs!"

She went off, and Bets was glad. "Her glasses fell off six times, Luke," she said.

"You're a caution, you are," said Luke. "I only hope she doesn't go and tell Mr. Tupping she saw you here!"

But that is just what Miss Trimble *did* do! She did not mean any harm. She did not even know that Tupping had ordered the children out of the garden some days before. She was picking roses the very next day, when Tupping came along behind her and stood watching her.

Miss Trimble began to feel scared, as she always did when the surly gardener came along. He was so rude. She turned and gave him a frightened smile.

"Lovely morning, Tupping, isn't it?" she said. "Beautiful roses these."

"Won't be beautiful long when you've finished messing about with them," said Tupping.

"Oh, I'm not spoiling them!" said Miss Trimble. "I know how to pick roses."

"You don't know any more than a child!" said surly Tupping, enjoying seeing how scared poor Miss Trimble was of him.

The mention of a child made Miss Trimble remember Bets. "Oh," she said, trying to turn the conversation away from roses – "oh, there was such a dear little girl with Luke in the garden yesterday!"

Tupping's face grew as black as thunder. "A girl here!" he shouted. "Where's that Luke? I'll skin him if he lets those kids in here whilst my back is turned!"

He went off to find Luke. Miss Trimble shook with fright, and her glasses fell off and got so entangled in her lace collar that it took quite twenty minutes for her trembling hands to disentangle them.

"A most unpleasant fellow!" she kept murmuring to herself. "Dear, dear! I hope I haven't got poor Luke into trouble. He's such a pleasant fellow – and only a boy too.· I do hope he won't get into trouble."

Luke *was* in trouble. Tupping strode up to him and glowered, his stone-coloured eyes almost hidden under his shaggy brows.

"Who was that girl in here yesterday?" he demanded. "One of them kids next door, was it? What was she doing here?"

"Nothing she shouldn't do, Mr. Tupping," said Luke. "She's a good little thing."

"I said *'What was she doing here?'* " shouted Mr. Tupping. "Taking the peaches, I suppose – or picking the plums!"

"She's the little girl from next door," said Luke hotly. "She wouldn't take nothing like that. I just gave her some strawberry runners for her garden, that's all. They'd have been burnt on the rubbish-heap, anyway!"

Mr. Tupping looked as if he was going to have a fit. To think that Luke should give anyone anything out of *his* garden! He really thought it was his garden, and not Lady Candling's. He didn't stop to think that Lady Candling would willingly give a little girl a few strawberry runners, for she was fond of children.

Tupping gave Luke a box on the ears, and went straight to the wall. Luke did not dare to follow him. He felt certain that all the children were out, because he had heard their voices and their bicycle bells some time back on the road. He stooped over his work, his ears red. He felt angry with Miss Trimble. Why had she given Bets away?

The children *had* gone out on their bicycles – all but Bets. The ride they were going was too far for her, so the little girl had been left behind with Buster, much to her annoyance. It was such a nuisance being four or five years younger than the others. They kept on leaving her out!

"Buster, come and sit by me and I'll read you a story

about rabbits," said Bets. At the word "Rabbits" Buster ran to Bets. He thought she was going to take him for a walk. But instead she sat down under a tree and took a book from under her arm. She opened it and began to read.

"Once there was a big, fat rabbit called Woffly. He . . ."

But Buster was bored. He got up and ran to the bottom of the drive waiting for the others to come back. Bets sat there alone. She suddenly heard a noise and looked up – and, oh dear me, there, climbing over the wall, looking as fierce as could be, was that horrid Mr. Tupping!

Tupping, Buster, And Mr. Goon

Bets was horrified. She couldn't even get up and run away. She looked round for Buster, but he wasn't there. She stared in fright at Mr. Tupping, who came towards her with a red and angry face.

"You the little girl who came into my garden yesterday?" he said.

Bets nodded. She couldn't say a word.

"Did you take my strawberry runners?" asked Mr. Tupping, even more fiercely.

Still Bets couldn't say a word. She nodded again, her face very white. Surely, surely, it hadn't been wrong to have those strawberry runners! She had planted them carefully in her little garden, and had watered them well. They were hers now. They would only have been thrown away and burnt.

Mr. Tupping put out his hand and jerked the frightened little girl to her feet. "You show me where you put them," he said.

"Let me go," said Bets, finding her tongue at last. "I'll tell Mummy about you!"

"You tell her if you like," said Mr. Tupping. "And

I'll tell Mr. Goon the policeman, see? I'll tell him you took my strawberry runners, and he'll put you and Luke into prison!"

"They don't put little girls into prison," sobbed Bets. But her heart went cold at the thought of Luke going to prison.

"Where's them strawberry runners?" demanded Mr. Tupping. Bets led him to her garden. As soon as Mr. Tupping saw the neatly-planted, well-watered little strawberry plants he bent down and wrenched every one of them up. He tore them up into tiny pieces and threw them on to the bonfire that was smouldering nearby. Bets sobbed bitterly. Poor little strawberry plants!

"You're a bad girl," said Mr. Tupping. "And I tell you this — if you come into my garden again, I'll go straight to Mr. Goon the policeman. Great friend of mine, he is, and he'll be along to see your father before you can say 'Jack Robinson.' As for that Luke — well, he'll end up in prison, no doubt about that."

With that Mr. Tupping began to walk back to the wall; but before he could get there, Buster came running up. He heard Bets sobbing, he smelt Mr. Tupping, and he put two and two together at once. Buster certainly had brains!

He flew straight at Tupping and caught him by the trouser-leg, growling in a most fearsome way. Mr. Tupping gave a howl.

"Call your dog off!" he yelled. Bets called Buster.

"Oh, Buster, don't! Come here, Buster!"

But Buster was having a lovely time. Here was his enemy ill-treating his beloved little Bets. Grrrrrrrrr!

Tupping was frightened. He kicked out and picked up a stick. Buster tore a large piece out of Tupping's trouser-leg, and retired under a bush to chew it. Tupping took his chance and shinned up the wall. Buster was out from the bush in a trice, snapping at Tupping's ankles, getting another bit of trouser and a nice piece of woollen sock too.

Tupping gave a yell, and fell off on the other side of the wall.

Bets was half-laughing and half-crying by now. "Oh, Buster, darling Buster, I think you're marvellous!" she said.

"Grrrrrrrr!" said Buster happily, still chewing a bit of trouser.

Bets sat down and thought. She longed to run in and tell her mother all about everything, and feel her mother's arms round her. The little girl had had a shock. But she was afraid that if she told her mother, Mummy would go and tell Lady Candling, and Lady Candling would scold Tupping, and Tupping would go to the police and say that Luke had stolen things to give to her, Bets.

"And Mr. Goon doesn't like us, ever since we solved the mystery of the burnt cottage before he did!" said Bets to herself. "So he would love to listen to everything that Tupping said and make a fuss about it. And Luke might really and truly be sent to prison. Oh, I do wish the others were here."

They came back at last. Fatty noticed Bet's tear-stained face at once.

"What's up?" he said. "Got into a row, little Bets?"

"Oh, an awful thing happened this morning," said Bets, glad to pour out everything to the others. She told them the whole story. The three boys went red with rage to think that little Bets should have been treated like that. Daisy put her arms round her and gave her a hug.

"Poor old Bets," she said. "Go on – what happened next?"

Then Bets told about Buster and how he had torn pieces out of Tupping's trouser-legs. The children roared with laughter, and gave Buster a great petting. "Good dog, good dog!" said Pip. "That's the stuff to give to surly old Tupping. Good dog!"

Fatty put his arm round Bets. "You did quite right not to tell your mother," he said. "I mean – it will save Luke a

31

lot of trouble if we keep this quiet, because he would be terribly scared if the policeman came to question him. You know what old Luke is – frightened of all grown-ups simply because most of them have been so beastly to him."

"Fancy tearing up Bet's plants like that," said Pip. "If I was old enough I'd go and shake Tupping till his teeth fell out!"

The others laughed. They all felt like that when they thought of poor frightened little Bets and her precious strawberry plants. Buster barked and wagged his tail.

"He says he did his best to give Tupping a shaking?" said Daisy.

The children did their best to make up to Bets for her fright. They were very kind to her. Larry went straight home, asked his mother if he might dig up a few strawberry plants for Bets, and brought them back. He planted them himself for her, and the little girl was very pleased.

Fatty brought her a book. He spent all his pocket-money on it, and never even said so, which was good for Fatty.

Daisy gave her one of her old dolls, which pleased Bets more than anything. Even Pip, who usually hadn't much time for his "baby-sister" as he called her, took her for a ride all round the garden on his big bicycle. So altogether Bets had a good time.

The children wondered if Luke had got into trouble. When they heard his familiar whistle at five o'clock they ran down to the gate to meet him as he went home.

"Luke! How did Tupping find out about Bets and the strawberry plants? Did you get into trouble? Did you know he scared Bets terribly?"

"Poor little Bets," said Luke. "I didn't know she was in, or I'd have gone after old Tupping. I thought you were all out. I heard your bicycle bells, you see. When Tupping came back and told me he'd gone for Bets, and torn up all her plants, I could have knocked him down. But he would only have reported me to Mr. Goon the policeman, so what would have been the good of that?"

"Did you get into an awful row?" asked Bets. "How did he find out about me?"

"Miss Tremble must have told him, the silly old thing," said Luke. "Yes, I did get into a row. I got my ears boxed, and I had to work harder than ever today. I wish I could leave."

"I wish you could, too," said Larry. "Why can't you?"

"Well, it's my first job you see, and you should stick in your first job as long as you can," said Luke. "And there's another thing – I bet Tupping would give me a bad name if I gave him notice, and I might not be able to get another job. Then I'd get into trouble with my stepfather. I give him half my money, you see."

"You have a lot of troubles, Luke," said Daisy. "I wish we could help you."

"Well, you do in a way," said Luke. "I tell you things, don't I? I don't keep them all bottled up like I used to. It's nice to tell them to somebody. Look, there's old Goon, the village bobby! "

Mr. Goon, burly, red-faced, with bulging frog-eyes, was walking down the lane towards the children.

"Do you suppose he is going to see Mr. Tupping?" asked Bets in alarm.

"Don't know," said Luke, also looking rather alarmed. He was afraid of policemen, and Mr. Goon was not a very nice one.

"I wonder if he'll tell us to clear orf," whispered Daisy. "Do you remember how often he shouted 'Clear orf! ' to us in the Easter holidays? Horrid old Clear-Orf! "

Mr. Goon came slowly towards them. The children watched him. Buster growled. Mr. Goon pretended not to notice any of them. He did not feel at all friendly towards the children since they had solved a mystery he had been unable to solve himself.

Buster suddenly flew round Mr. Goon and barked madly at his ankles. He did not attempt to bite him or snap at him, but he startled Mr. Goon all the same.

"Clear orf!" said Mr. Goon to Buster, in a threatening tone. "Do you hear? Clear orf!"

"Buster, come here!" said Fatty, but not in a very commanding voice. Buster took no notice. He was having a lovely day. First Mr. Tupping and now Mr. Goon to frighten. Oh, what a treat for a little black Scottie!

"Clear ORF," said Mr. Goon. Luke gave one of his loud laughs as Buster jumped nimbly out of the way of a kick. The policeman looked at him.

"Ho, you!" he said, "you'll get into trouble, you will, if you laugh at the Law. What you doing here? You clear orf!"

"He's our friend," said Fatty. "Come here, Buster!"

Mr. Tupping, hearing the noise of barking and shouting, appeared at the other gate of the drive. He knew Buster at once.

"You'd better report that there dog," remarked Mr. Tupping to the policeman. "Tore a bit out of me trousers today – look here! Vicious dog, that's what he is. Right-down vicious."

He caught sight of Luke. "What you doing hanging about here instead of going home?" he asked. Luke disappeared at once, going off up the lane quickly. He wanted no more trouble from either Mr. Tupping or Mr. Goon.

Buster returned from the battle and went to Fatty, who picked him up.

"Right-down vicious dog," said Mr. Tupping again. "If you want any details, Mr. Goon, I'll give you them."

Mr. Goon did not want to report Buster, because he knew that any report would go before Inspector Jenks, who was very friendly with the children. Still, he thought there would be no harm in pretending that he *was* going to report Buster for being vicious and out of control, so he pulled out his big black notebook, took his stubby pencil and began to write solemnly and slowly.

The children were rather alarmed. They all went back

into Pip's garden at once. Bets gazed at Buster, her eyes wide with fright.

"Would they – would they put Buster in prison?" she asked fearfully – and was very much relieved when all the others burst out laughing.

"Of course not," said Fatty. "Nobody ever heard of a dog's prison, Bets. Don't you worry about old Buster!"

Dark Queen Disappears

Things began to happen very quickly after this, and, quite suddenly, the Five Find-Outers found that there was a first-class mystery for them to solve.

The next afternoon Pip's mother, Mrs. Hilton, went to tea with Lady Candling, who was now back again next door after a short holiday.

"You may all have a picnic tea in the garden," she told Pip. "Daisy, see that everyone behaves, please, and if you haven't enough to eat, go and ask Cook politely – *politely*, remember – for some more bread-and-butter."

"Yes, Mrs. Hilton. Thank you very much," said Daisy. The children watched Pip's mother going down the drive at half-past three that afternoon, looking very smart. They were glad that *they* did not have to dress up and go out to tea. It was much more fun to have a picnic tea and wear old shorts and shirts!

They had a lovely tea, and went in twice to ask Cook for some more bread-and-butter. Daisy went, and remembered to ask very politely. There were ripe plums and greengages as well to eat, so it was a good tea.

Soon after tea Mrs. Hilton came back. She went straight to the children, looking rather worried.

"Children," she said, "what do you think has happened? That lovely prize-cat, called Dark Queen, has disappeared! Lady Candling is very upset, because she is most valuable. And the dreadful thing is – Luke may have stolen her!"

"*Mother!*" said Pip indignantly, "Luke's our friend. He would never, never do a thing like that!"

"He wouldn't, he wouldn't!" cried Bets.

"Oh, Mrs. Hilton," said Fatty earnestly, "I really don't think you are right in saying that Luke did that!"

"I didn't say he *had*," said Mrs. Hilton. "I said that he might have. All the evidence points to the fact that he was about the only one who could have done so."

"But he couldn't, he simply couldn't," said Daisy. "He's as honest as the day. It is much more likely to have been that hateful old Tupping."

"Tupping has been out all the afternoon with Mr. Goon the policeman, who appears to be his friend," said Mrs. Hilton. "So it is quite impossible that he could have stolen her."

The children stared at Mrs. Hilton, feeling upset and puzzled. Fatty took command of the whole affair, and spoke politely to Mrs. Hilton.

"Luke is a very good friend of ours, Mrs. Hilton, and if he is in trouble we must help him. I am quite sure he had nothing to do with Dark Queen disappearing, nothing at all. Could you please give us the whole story? This looks like something the Five Find-Outers can tackle again."

"My dear Frederick, don't talk so pompously," said Mrs. Hilton rather impatiently. "And don't start interfering in this matter, for goodness' sake. It's nothing to do with you. Just because you solved one mystery quite well is no reason why you should think you can interfere in anything else that crops up."

Fatty went red. He didn't like being ticked off in public like that.

"Mother, please do tell us all that has happened," said Pip.

"Well," said Mrs. Hilton, "Miss Harmer went off for

the day this morning, after feeding all the cats and cleaning out their cages. Dark Queen was in the big cage with the other cats today. Miss Harmer went to catch the ten o'clock bus. Miss Trimble went with Lady Candling to see that the cats were all right at just before one o'clock, and Tupping pointed out Dark Queen to them. You know what a beauty she is."

The children nodded. "Go on, Mother," said Pip. "Was that the last time that anyone saw Dark Queen?"

"No," said his mother. "Miss Trimble went with me to show me the cats at four o'clock, just before tea — and Dark Queen was there then, in the cage with the others."

"How do you know, Mother?" asked Pip. "How could you tell which was Dark Queen? They are all exactly alike."

"I know," said Mrs. Hilton, "but apparently Dark Queen has been bitten on the tail, and a few hairs there grew cream instead of dark-brown. Miss Trimble pointed out the cat to me and I remember noticing the ring of creamy hairs — most noticeable. So she was in the cage, quite safe, at four o'clock."

"Go on," said Pip.

"Tupping came back at five o'clock and he brought Mr. Goon the village policeman with him," said Mrs. Hilton. "He showed Mr. Goon his prize tomatoes, and then he showed him the cats. Then Mr. Tupping suddenly noticed that Dark Queen was missing!"

"Gracious!" said Fatty. "Then the cat must have disappeared between four and five o'clock, Mrs. Hilton."

"Yes," said Pip's mother. "And as Luke was the only one in the garden, I am afraid that he is suspected. He knew that the cat was worth a lot of money. Tupping says that the boy stole something the other day too — strawberry runners or something silly like that."

Bets went fiery red. Tears came into her eyes. Those awful strawberry runners! She wondered if she should

37

tell her mother about them, but Fatty frowned at her, warning her not to.

"Well, that's all," said Mrs. Hilton, pulling off her gloves. "But I'm afraid your friend Luke is in for trouble now. I wonder where he took the cat. No one seems to have seen Luke between four and five o'clock, so I suppose he could have put her into a basket and taken her off anywhere."

"Mummy, Luke wouldn't!" burst out Bets. "You don't know how kind and honest he is. He gave me a lot of whistles he made – and this lovely model of Dark Queen too. Look!"

"I wish you wouldn't make such extraordinary friends," said her mother, not looking at the model at all. "You are none of you old enough to know whether anyone is really honest or not. Please don't talk to Luke any more."

Mrs. Hilton went towards the house and disappeared indoors. The children looked at one another in dismay.

"It's just no good to say, 'Don't talk to Luke any more,'" said Fatty. "We've simply got to. He's our friend, and he's helped us lots of times – and Buster too. We've got to help *him* now."

All the others agreed. They sat and thought about everything for a little, and then began to talk about it.

"*Some*body must have stolen Dark Queen, there's no doubt about that," said Fatty. "It seems as if it could only be old Luke; but we're all absolutely certain it isn't, so who else could it be?"

"Let's look for clues!" said Bets eagerly, remembering how exciting it had been to look for clues in the last mystery they had solved.

"Let's draw up a list of Suspects!" said Daisy. "We did that before."

"Now," said Fatty importantly, "it seems to me that the Five Find-Outers can really get to work again. I propose. . . ."

"Look here," said Larry, "you're forgetting something, Fatty. *I'm* head of the Find-Outers, not you."

"All right," said Fatty, looking sulky. "Go ahead then. Only I've got far more brains than you have. I was top of my form last term, and. . . ."

"Shut up, Fatty," said everyone together, except Bets. Fatty looked as if he was going to get up and go; but he was too excited and interested to be sulky for long, and soon the five children were eagerly discussing their plans.

"Now, let's think everything out clearly," said Daisy.

"Dark Queen was with the others until four o'clock, because it was then that Miss Tremble and Pip's mother saw her. She wasn't there when Clear-Orf and Tupping went to see them at five. So, in that hour, somebody must have gone to the cage, unlocked it, taken out the cat, locked the cage again, and gone off with Dark Queen, and either given her to someone else or hidden her away."

"Right," said Larry. "Very clearly put, Daisy."

"The next thing is: Who could have stolen the cat? Whom can we suspect?" said Pip.

"Well, I suppose Miss Tremble might have slipped down and taken Dark Queen out," said Fatty. "Not very likely, of course, because Miss Tremble, poor thing, is the kind of person who would have a fit if she even posted a letter without a stamp. She'd dream about it all night long! Still, we have to consider everyone who had a *chance* of stealing Dark Queen."

Larry pulled out a notebook. "I'll write the names down, he said. "Miss Tremble is one. What about Lady Candling?"

"She wouldn't steal her own cat, silly," said Daisy.

"She might," said Larry. "It might be insured against theft, you know. She would get a lot of money. You've got to think of all these things." He wrote down Lady Candling's name.

"Tupping?" said Bets.

Larry shook his head very regretfully. "No, Bets. I'd love to put his name down; but if he was with old Clear-Orf all the afternoon it's just no good suspecting him. What about Miss Harmer? Could she possibly have come back quietly and secretly from her day out and taken the cat? She knew how valuable Dark Queen was."

This was quite a new idea. Everyone thought of the plump, smiling Miss Harmer. She didn't seem at all the sort of person who would steal a valuable cat from her employer. Still – her name went down on the list of Suspects.

"We'll have to try and find out where Miss Harmer was between four and five o'clock today," said Pip.

"Who else is there?" said Daisy. "We've got Miss Tremble, Lady Candling, and Miss Harmer down. What about the cook and house-parlourmaid next door? They would have had a chance of going down to the cat-house and taking Dark Queen, wouldn't they?"

"I've never seen the cook or parlourmaid," said Pip. "None of us have. We'll have to find out about them too. Goodness, we've got quite a lot of suspected people after all! We'll have a lot of work to do!"

"The one person who is horrid enough to have done it is Tupping – and he's just the very one we can't even suspect," said Bets sadly. "Well, there aren't any more Suspects, are there?"

"We'll have to put old Luke down," said Larry. "I know we *don't* suspect him – but Tupping has accused him of the crime, so we'd better put him down. We can cross him out as soon as we like."

So Luke's name went down too. Poor old Luke! He always seemed to be in trouble.

"Let's go and whistle to him," said Larry. "He hasn't gone home yet, or he'd have whistled to us and told us everything."

So they went to the wall and whistled the special notes

that they and Luke used for signalling to one another. But although they whistled and whistled, nobody came. Whatever could Luke be doing?

Luke gets into Trouble

The five children sat on top of the wall, with Buster scratching at the bricks below. They wondered what to do. Pip looked at his watch.

"Just gone quarter to six," he said. "*Can* Luke have gone home? No; he surely would have spoken to us first."

"Perhaps old Clear-Orf is questioning him," said Fatty. This seemed very likely. The children wished they could find out.

Fatty had a good idea. "Look here, Pip," he said, "*you* could find out what's happening if you liked."

"How?" asked Pip.

"Well, your mother has just been to tea next door, hasn't she," said Fatty. "You could hop over the wall, and go and see what's happening; and if anyone sees you and wants to know what you are doing there, you could say your mother has just been to tea, and has she by any chance dropped her hanky in the garden?"

"But she hasn't," said Pip. "Didn't you see her take it out of her bag when she was talking to us? It had a most lovely smell."

"Of course I did, idiot," said Fatty impatiently. "It's only just an excuse. You don't need to say she *did* drop her hanky, because we know she didn't – but you could easily say, 'Had she?' couldn't you?"

"It's a good idea of Fatty's," said Larry. "It's about the only way any of us could get into the garden without being sent out at once by Clear-Orf or Tupping. Go on, Pip. Jump down and see whether you can find out what's

41

happening. Hurry up. It's really a great bit of luck that your mother has just been there to tea."

Pip was anxious to go – and yet very much afraid of meeting Tupping or Clear-Orf. He jumped down, waved to the others, and set off through the bushes.

There was no sign of Luke at all. Pip passed by the cat-house, but there was no one there either. He peeped into the cage where Dark Queen should have been with the others. The cats looked at him and mewed. Pip went on down the path, round by the greenhouses, and then stood hidden in the bushes. He could hear voices nearby.

He peeped through the bushes. There was a little group of people on the lawn. Pip knew most of them.

"There's Lady Candling," he thought. "And that's Miss Tremble – doesn't she look upset! And there's Tupping, looking very pleased and important – and that's old Clear-Orf the bobby! And oh, there's poor old Luke!"

Poor Luke was there, in the centre, looking quite bewildered and terribly scared. The policeman was standing opposite to him, big black notebook in hand, and Luke was stammering and stuttering out replies to questions that Mr. Goon was barking out at him.

At the back were two maids, plainly the cook and the parlourmaid, both looking excited. They were whispering together, nudging one another.

Pip crept nearer. He could hear the questions now that were fired at poor frightened Luke.

"What were you doing all the afternoon?"

"I was – I was – digging up the old peas – in the Long Bed," stammered Luke.

"Is that the bed by the cat-house?" asked Mr. Goon, scribbling something down in his book.

"Y-y-y-yes, sir," stuttered Luke.

"So you were by the cats the whole afternoon?" said the policeman. "Did anyone come near them?"

"Miss T-t-tremble came at f-f-four o'clock about, with another l-l-lady," said Luke, pushing back his untidy hair. "They stayed a few minutes and went."

"And what did *you* do between four and five o'clock?" said Mr. Goon in a very threatening sort of voice.

Luke looked as if he was going to fall down in terror. "N-n-nothing, sir – only d-d-d-dug!" he stammered. "Just d-d-d-dug – alongside the cat-house. And nobody came near, not a soul, till you and Mr. Tupping came along to see the cats."

"*And* we found that Dark Queen was gone," said Mr. Tupping in a fierce voice. "Well, Mr. Goon – the evidence is as plain as plain, isn't it? He took that cat – no doubt about it – and handed her to some friend of his for a bit of pocket-money. He's a bad boy is Luke, and always has been ever since I had him."

"I'm not bad, Mr. Tupping!" shouted Luke, suddenly finding a little courage. "I've never took a thing I shouldn't! I've worked hard for you! I've stood things from you I shouldn't stand. You know I'd never steal one of them cats. I'd be too scared to, even if I thought of it!"

"That's enough, now, that's enough," said Mr. Goon fiercely. "Don't you go talking to Mr. Tupping like that. What boys like you want is a good hiding."

"Ah, I'll see he gets it all right," said Mr. Tupping in a horrid voice. "I'll have a word with his stepfather. *He* knows what this lad's like, right enough."

"I think, Tupping," said Lady Candling in her low, clear voice, "I think there is no need to say anything to Luke's stepfather until we know a little more about this curious happening."

Tupping looked rather taken aback. He had been enjoying himself so much that he had half-forgotten Lady Candling was there. Luke turned to his mistress.

"Please, Mam," he said in an urgent voice, "please, Mam, I do beg of you not to believe what Mr. Tupping and Mr. Goon say about me. I didn't take Dark Queen. I don't know where she is. I've never taken a thing I shouldn't take from your garden!"

"And that's a lie!" said Mr. Tupping in a triumphant voice. *"What about them strawberry runners?"*

To Pip's horror, poor Luke, now frightened and upset beyond bearing, burst into enormous sobs that shook his big body in an alarming manner. He put his arm across his face, trying to hide it.

"Let him go home," said Lady Candling in a gentle voice. "You have questioned him enough. He's only a fifteen-year-old boy, after all. Mr. Goon, I ask you to go now, please, and Luke, you may go home too."

Mr. Goon didn't look at all pleased. He was sorry he could not treat Luke as he would have treated a grown man. He knew he would have to let him go home. He didn't like being sent off himself by Lady Candling either. He cleared his throat loudly, gave Lady Candling a scornful look, and shut his notebook.

"I must have a few words with your stepfather," he said in a pompous tone to Luke, who turned very pale at these words. He was very much afraid of his stepfather.

"I'll walk down with you," said Mr. Tupping. "It's possible that the boy's father may tell us something about his friends. He must have given Dark Queen to one of them."

So poor Luke was marched off between Mr. Goon and Mr. Tupping, still giving enormous sobs now and then. Pip hated the policeman and the gardener. Poor Luke! What could he do against two men like that? There just wasn't a chance for him!

Pip didn't know that the two were taking Luke down nearby where he was hiding, and he didn't step back into the thick bushes in time to prevent himself from being seen. Mr. Tupping suddenly saw the boy's face peering out from a rhododendron bush.

He stopped, stepped swiftly into the bushes, grabbed hold of Pip, and pulled him out on to the path.

44

He grabbed Pip and pulled him out

"What are *you* doing here?" he roared. "It's one of them kids next door, Mr. Goon," he said to the surprised policeman. "Always poking in here. I'll march him straight off to her ladyship, and she'll give him a good talking-to!"

Luke stood staring open-mouthed as Pip was pushed roughly up the path by the angry gardener. Lady Candling had heard the noise, and had turned back to the lawn to see whatever was happening now!

"Let me go," said Pip angrily. "You hateful thing, let me go! You're hurting my arm!"

Tupping was twisting the boy's arm on purpose, and Pip knew it. But he couldn't possibly get away. Soon they were in front of Lady Candling, who looked extremely surprised.

"Found this boy hiding in the bushes," said Tupping. "Always finding them children in here. Friends of Luke, they are. Up to no good, I'll be bound!"

"What were you doing in my garden?" asked Lady Candling in rather a stern tone.

"My mother has just been to tea with you, Lady Candling," said Pip in his most polite voice. "I suppose you haven't by any chance found a handkerchief of hers left behind, have you?"

"Dear me! Are you Mrs. Hilton's son Philip?" asked Lady Candling, smiling at him. "She was telling me about you, and you have a little sister, haven't you, called Bets?"

"Yes, Lady Candling," said Pip, smiling sweetly too. "She's a dear little girl. I'd like to bring her in to see you some day if I may."

"Yes, do," said Lady Candling. "Tupping, you have made a stupid mistake. This little boy quite obviously came in to look for his mother's handkerchief. Mrs. Hilton was at tea with me today."

Pip rubbed his arm hard, screwing up his face as if it hurt him. "Did Tupping hurt you?" said Lady Candling.

"I'm really very sorry. Tupping, you seem to have been very rough with this child."

Tupping scowled. Things were not going at all the way he had expected.

"If we find your mother's handkerchief we will certainly send it in," said Lady Candling to Pip. "And do remember to bring in your little sister to see me, won't you? I am very fond of little girls."

"Tupping will turn us out if we come," said Pip.

"Indeed he won't!" said Lady Candling at once. "Tupping, the children are to come in when they wish to. Those are my orders."

Tupping's face went red, and he looked as if he was going to burst. But he did not dare to say anything to his mistress. He turned rudely, and went back to Mr. Goon and Luke, who were waiting some way off.

Pip shook hands with Lady Candling, thanked her, said good-bye, and went after Tupping.

"Luke!" he called. "Luke! Don't give up hope! All your friends will help you! *We* know you didn't do it!"

"You clear orf!" said Mr. Goon, now really angry. "None of your sauce! Always poking your nose in and interfering! Clear orf, I say!"

But Pip didn't clear off. Keeping just beyond Mr. Goon's reach he danced along behind the three, shouting encouraging messages to Luke, and annoying the policeman and the gardener beyond measure.

He heard Mr. Goon say to Mr. Tupping that he would return later in the evening to have a "good look round that cat-house."

"Oh," thought Pip, "he's going to hunt for clues to help him to put the blame on Luke. *We'd* better go hunting for clues first. I'll go and tell the others."

So, with a last hearty yell to Luke, Pip ran for the wall, climbed it, and rushed to tell the others all that he had heard. Things were getting really exciting!

"What happened, Pip? You've been simply ages and ages!" said Larry, as Pip flung himself down beside the four children and Buster.

"Oh, Clear-Orf and Tupping have quite made up their minds that Luke Did the Deed," said Pip.

"It's funny, isn't it?" said Bets, puzzled. "We know quite well that Luke didn't do it – and yet it seems as if he simply must have! It's a real, proper mystery."

"I wonder where Dark Queen *is*," said Bets.

"Yes. If we could find her, we should have a better idea of who stole her," said Larry. "I mean, whoever has her now must be a friend of the thief. Golly! this *is* a puzzle, isn't it?"

"Can't we look for clues?" asked Bets, thinking that perhaps this might help to clear Luke.

"Oh, that reminds me," said Pip at once. "Old Clear-Orf said he was coming back tonight to have a look round the cat-house. I expect he wants to find some clues himself – clues that will point to poor old Luke, I suppose!"

"Well, I vote we go and have a look first," said Fatty at once, getting up.

"What, go over the wall now!" said Larry in surprise. "We'll get into trouble."

"We shan't," said Fatty. "We'll be gone long before Tupping and Clear-Orf get back. They'll be having a fine time telling poor old Luke's stepfather all about him."

"All right. Let's go now then," said Larry. "We might be able to find some sort of clue, though goodness knows what! Come on."

Buster was left behind; and this time he was put into the shed and locked up there, so that he wouldn't go rushing down Pip's drive and up Lady Candling's to find them!

They all climbed over the wall, Fatty giving Bets a helping hand. There didn't seem to be anyone about. The children made their way cautiously to the cat-house. The cats lay lazily on their benches, their blue eyes blinking at the children.

"Now," said Larry, "look for clues."

"What sort of clues?" whispered Bets.

"Don't know till we see some," said Larry. "Look on the ground – and all round about. See! this is where old Luke must have been working this afternoon."

The boy pointed to where a barrow stood half full of weeds. A spade was stuck in the ground. Luke's coat hung on a tree nearby.

"He was digging over that bed," said Fatty thoughtfully. "He couldn't have been working any nearer to the cat-house than that! He would have seen anyone coming or going to the cats, wouldn't he? He couldn't have helped it. The children went and stood where Luke had been working. They could see every cat from where they stood. It would surely have been impossible to take a cat out, and lock the door, without being seen by Luke.

And yet a cat had gone, and Luke swore *he* hadn't stolen her – so who in the wide world could have taken Dark Queen?

"Let's look all round the cat-house and see if the cat could have escaped by herself," said Larry suddenly.

"Good idea," said Fatty. So they walked all round the strongly-built wooden houses, which were set high on stout wooden legs, rather like modern hen-houses.

"There's absolutely nowhere that a cat could get out," said Pip. "Not a hole the size of a small mouse even! Dark Queen certainly couldn't have escaped. She was taken out by somebody. That's certain."

"I say – what's that?" Pip pointed to something that lay on the floor of the big cage in which all the cats lived. the children peered through the wire-netting at it.

There was a short silence. Then Fatty pursed up his lips, raised his eyebrows, and scratched his head.

"Blow!" he said. "I know what that is! It's one of those cunning little whistles that Luke is always making for Bets."

It was. There it lay on the cage-floor, a most tiresome and shocking clue. How could it have got there? Only one way – Luke must have been inside the cage and dropped the whistle. All the children felt suddenly puzzled and shocked.

"It wasn't Luke; it wasn't, it wasn't," said Bets, with tears in her voice. "We all know it wasn't."

"Yes. We all know it wasn't. And yet there in the cage is a whistle that only Luke could have dropped," said Fatty. "This is a very extraordinary mystery, I must say."

"Fatty, if Mr. Goon sees that whistle, will he say it's a proper proof that Luke was the thief?" asked Bets anxiously.

Fatty nodded. "Of course. It's a most enormous, unmistakable clue, Bets – to someone like Clear-Orf, who can't see farther than his nose."

"But it isn't a clue like that to you, is it, Fatty?" went on Bets, clutching his hand. "Oh, Fatty! you don't think Luke dropped it, do you?"

"I'll tell you what I think," said Fatty. "I think that somebody put it there so that Luke might be suspected. That's what I think."

"Golly! I think you're right!" said Larry. "This is getting very mysterious. I say, do you think we ought to leave this clue for Clear-Orf to see? After all, we're pretty certain it's a false clue, aren't we?"

"You're right," said Pip. "I vote we get the clue out, and take it away!"

The five children stared at the whistle lying on the floor. The cage was locked. The key was gone. How could they get the whistle out?

"We'll have to be quick," said Fatty desperately. "Clear-Orf may be back in a short while. For goodness' sake! how can we get that whistle out of the cage?"

Nobody knew. If the whistle had been a little nearer the wire-netting, the children might have got some wire or a stick and worked it near enough to take out. But it was at the back of the cage.

Then Fatty had one of his brain-waves. He picked up a small pebble and shot it into the cage, so that it rolled near the little whistle. One of the cats saw the pebble rolling and jumped down to play with it. She put out a paw and patted the pebble. Her paw touched the whistle and moved it. She began to play with the wooden whistle too.

The children watched breathlessly. The cat sent the pebble rolling away and went after it. Then she came back to the whistle and looked hard at it, as if she expected it to move.

Then out went her paw again and she gave the whistle a push. It rolled over and over and the cat was delighted. She picked the whistle up cleverly in her two front paws, juggled with it a little, then let it drop. She struck it with her paw, and it flew through the air, landing quite near to the wire netting.

"Oh, good, good, good!" said Fatty joyfully. He took a small roll of wire from his pocket. It was wonderful the things that Fatty kept in his pockets. He undid a length of the wire, twisted two pieces together, and made a small loop at one end. Then he pushed the wire through one of the holes in the netting.

Everyone watched eagerly. The wire reached the whistle. Fatty jiggled it about patiently, trying to fit the loop at the end over the whistle. The cat that had played with the whistle watched with great interest. Then suddenly it put out a playful paw and patted the wire, sending the loop neatly over the whistle!

"Oh, thanks, puss!" said Fatty gleefully, and drew the whistle carefully to the wire-netting. He jerked it up, and the whistle flew through one of the holes and landed at Bets' feet. She picked it up.

"Got it!" said Fatty. "Let's have a look at it. Yes, it's one of Luke's all right. What a good thing we got it out. Now that clue won't be found by old Clear-Orf! Luke won't get into further trouble because of *that*!"

"You really are clever, Fatty," said Bets, in the greatest admiration.

"Good work, Fatty," said Pip.

Fatty at once swelled up with pride and importance. "Oh, that's nothing," he began. "I've often had better ideas than this. Why, once . . ."

"Shut up!" said Larry, Daisy, and Pip together. Fatty shut up. He stuffed the whistle into his pocket.

"Look about for any more clues," said Pip. "There might be some more in the cage."

The five of them pressed their noses once more to the cage netting. Bets wrinkled up her nose.

"I don't like the smell in the cage," she said.

"Well, animals never smell very nice when they are caged," said Larry.

"No, it's another smell," said Bets. "Like petrol or something."

The all sniffed. "She means turpentine," said Fatty. "I can smell it too – quite faintly. Afraid that's not a clue though, Bets. Still, it's good to notice even a smell. Perhaps Miss Harmer uses turps to clean out the cage. Now – any other clue, anybody?"

But there really did not seem to be anything at all to be found, although the children hunted around the cages and peered inside them time and again.

"Sickening," said Fatty. "Nothing to help us at all. Not a thing. Well, it's a jolly good thing we found that whistle before Tupping or Clear-Orf spotted it. I feel certain somebody put it there so that Luke might be suspected of stealing the cat. What a mean trick to play!"

"I wish *we* could put a whole lot of clues in the cage so

that it would muddle up old Clear-Orf," said Pip.

The others stared at him in delight, the same delicious thought striking them all at the same moment.

"Golly, what a marvellous idea! " said Fatty, wishing he had thought of it himself.

"Yes; let's do it! " said Larry excitedly. "Let's put all kinds of silly clues, that couldn't possibly point to Luke. It will give old Clear-Orf a most frightful headache sorting them all out! "

They all began to giggle. What should they push into the cage?

"I've got some peppermint drops," said Pip, with a chuckle. "I'll chuck one into the cage."

"And I'll put a piece of my hair-ribbon in," said Daisy. "It tore in half today and I've got the bits in my pocket. I'll put a half-bit in through the wire! "

"And I've got some blue buttons off my doll's coat," said Bets. "I'll put one of those in! "

"I believe I've got a new pair of brown shoe-laces somewhere in my pocket," said Larry, digging about in his shorts pockets. "Yes, here they are. I'll put one into the cage."

"What will you put in, Fatty?" asked Bets.

Fatty produced a collection of cigar-ends out of his pocket. The others stared at them in amazement.

"What do you want to collect cigar-ends for?" asked Larry at last.

"I smoke them," said Fatty. "They're the ends of the cigars my father smokes. He leaves them on the ash-tray in his bedroom."

"You *don't* smoke them! " said Pip disbelievingly. "You're just saying that to swank as usual. You just take them to make yourself smell of grown-up cigar-smoke, that's all. I often wondered why you smelt like that."

This was rather too near the truth for Fatty's liking. He pretended not to hear what Pip said. "I shall throw a cigar-end *under* the cage – on the ground," he said, "and one inside the cage – though I hope none of the cats will chew it and get ill. *Two* cigar-ends will just about send old Clear-Orf off his head."

Very solemnly the five children spread their "clues." Pip threw a large round peppermint drop into the cage, where the cats eyed it with displeasure. They evidently disapproved of the smell.

Daisy stuffed half a bit of rather grubby blue hair-ribbon into the netting. Bets put in a small blue button. Larry pushed in one of his new brown shoe-laces – and Fatty threw a cigar-end under the cage and one inside as well!

"There," he said, "plenty of clues for old Clear-Orf to find! Hope he comes soon."

Mr. Goon on the Job

"I say," said Daisy suddenly, watching her hair-ribbon flap on the floor of the cage, in a little draught from under the door. "I say, I hope no one will think *I*'ve stolen the cat! Mother would know that was a piece of my hair-ribbon if ever she saw it."

"Oh, crumbs! I never thought of that," said Pip.

"It's all right," said Fatty. "I've got a big envelope here – see? Now then, let's each put into the envelope the same thing that we've already settled for clues. I'll put in two cigar-ends, to match the ones I've left. Daisy, put in your other half of ribbon."

Daisy did so. Then Bets put in one of the blue doll's buttons, Larry put in the other shoe-lace, and Pip put in a peppermint drop.

Fatty folded up the envelope carefully and put it into his pocket. "If any of us is accused of the theft, because of the clues we've put in the cage, we've only got to show them what's in this envelope for them to know we did it for a joke," he said.

A bell rang out in Pip's house, and Bets gave a groan. "That's my bed-time bell. Blow! I don't want to go."

"You must," said Pip. "You got into a row yesterday for being late. Oh dear, I do wish we could stay here and see old Clear-Orf and Tupping finding the clues we've left!"

"Well, let's," said Larry.

"Oh, me too!" wailed Bets, afraid of being left out again. Pip give her a push.

"Bets, you *must* go! There's your bell again."

"Well, it's your bell too – it means you've got to come in and wash and change into your suit for supper-time," said Bets. "You know it does."

Pip did know it. Larry gave a sigh. He knew that he and Daisy ought to go home too. They had farther to go than Pip and Bets.

"We'll have to go too," said Larry. "Fatty, I suppose you couldn't possibly stay and watch, could you? It really would be funny to see. Why don't you stay? Your mother and father don't bother about you much, do they? You seem to go home or go out just whenever you like."

"All right, I'll stay here and watch," said Fatty. "I think I'll climb that tree there. It's easy to climb, and the leaves are nice and thick. I can see everything well from up there, and not be seen myself."

"Well, come on then, Bets," said Pip, not at all wanting to go. Fatty was going to have all the fun.

Then there came the sound of men's voices up the garden, and the children looked at one another at once.

"It's Tupping and Clear-Orf coming back," whispered Larry. "Over the wall, quick!"

"Good-bye, Fatty, see you tomorrow sometime," said Pip in a low voice. The four ran quietly to the wall. Pip gave Bets a leg-up, and got her safely over. The others were soon safely on the other side. Fatty was left by himself. He shinned up the tree very quickly, considering his plumpness.

Fatty sat on a broad bough, and carefully parted the leaves so that he could see what was going on down below. He saw Mr. Tupping coming towards the cat-house with Clear-Orf.

"Well now," Clear-Orf said, "we'll just have a look-round, Mr. Tupping. You never know when there's clues about, you know. Ah, many a clue I've found that's led me straight to the criminal."

"Ah!" said Mr. Tupping wisely, "I believe you, Mr. Goon. Well, I shouldn't be surprised if that boy Luke hasn't left something behind. He may be clever enough to steal a valuable cat, but he wouldn't be clever enough to hide his tracks."

The two men began to hunt carefully round and about the cat-house. The Siamese cats watched them out of brilliant blue eyes. They could not imagine why so many people came to their shed that day. Fatty looked down at the hunters, carefully peering between the leaves.

Mr. Goon found the cigar-end under the cat-house first. He pounced on it swiftly and held it up.

"What's that?" asked Mr. Tupping in astonishment.

"Cigar-end," said Mr. Goon with great satisfaction. Then he looked puzzled and tilted back his helmet to scratch his head. "Does that boy Luke smoke cigars?" he asked.

"Don't be silly," said Mr. Tupping impatiently. "'Course not. That's not a clue. Somebody who came with Lady Candling to see her cats must have chucked his cigar-end away under the house. That's all."

"Hmmm!" said Mr. Goon, not at all wanting to dismiss the cigar-end like that. "Well, I'll have to think about that."

Fatty giggled to himself. The two men went on searching. Mr. Tupping straightened himself up at last.

"Don't seem nothing else to be found," he said. "I

suppose there wouldn't be anything in the cat-house to see, do you think?"

Mr. Goon looked doubtful. "Shouldn't think so," he said. "But we might look. Got the key, Mr. Tupping?"

Mr. Tupping took the key down from a nail at the back of the cat-house. But before he had unlocked the door Mr. Goon gave a loud exclamation. He had looked through the wire-netting of the cat-house and had seen various things on the floor that caused him great excitement. Why, the place seemed alive with clues!

"What's up?" asked Mr. Tupping.

"Coo! Look here! See that shoe-lace there?" said Mr. Goon, pointing. "That's a whopping big clue, that is. Somebody's been in there and lost his shoe-lace!"

Mr. Tupping stared at the shoe-lace in the greatest astonishment. Then he saw the blue button – and the hair-ribbon. He gave a gasp of surprise. He inserted the key in the lock and opened the door.

The two men collected the "clues" from the cat-house. They brought them out to look at them.

"Whoever went in there wore shoes with brown laces, that's certain," said Mr. Goon with great satisfaction. "And look at that there button – that's come off somebody's coat, that has."

"What's this?" asked Mr. Tupping, showing Mr. Goon Pip's peppermint drop. Mr. Goon sniffed at it.

"Peppermint!" he said. "Now, does that boy Luke suck peppermints?"

"I expect so," said Mr. Tupping. "Most boys eat sweets. But Luke don't wear a hair-ribbon, Mr. Goon. And look, there's another cigar-end – like the one you found under the house."

Mr. Goon soon lost his excitement over his finds, and became puzzled. He gazed at his clues in silence.

"Judging by these here clues, the thief ought by rights to be someone that smokes cigars, wears blue hair-ribbons and blue buttons, sucks peppermint drops, and has brown laces in his shoes," he said. "It don't make sense."

Fatty was trying his hardest not to giggle out aloud. It was so funny seeing Mr. Goon and Mr. Tupping puzzle their heads over all the clues that the children had so carefully left for them to find. Mr. Goon cautiously licked the peppermint drop.

"Yes; it's peppermint right enough," he said. "Well, this is a fair puzzler – finding all these clues, and nobody we can fit them to, so to speak. You finding anything else, Mr. Tupping?"

Mr. Tupping had gone into the cat-house, and was looking all round it again very, very carefully.

"Just looking to see if there's any clue we've overlooked," he said. But he couldn't seem to find anything else, however hard he hunted. He came out again, looking rather untidy and cross.

"Well, there don't seem much else to be found," he said, sounding very disappointed. "I'm sure you'll find it's that boy Luke, Mr. Goon, that's the thief. These clues can't be clues – just things that got into the cage by accident."

"Well, a peppermint drop seems a funny sort of thing to get into the cage by accident," said Mr. Goon grumpily. "I'll have to take all these things home and think about them."

Fatty chuckled deep down in himself as he watched Mr. Goon put his "clues" into a clean white envelope, lick it up, write something on it, and put it carefully into his pocket. He turned to Mr. Tupping.

"Well, so long!" he said. "Thanks for your help. It's that boy Luke, no doubt about it. I've told him I'll go along and give him a thorough questioning tomorrow, and if I don't force a confession out of him, my name's not Theophilus Goon!"

And with that mouthful of a name old Clear-Orf departed majestically down the path, his "clues" safely in his pocket, his mind puzzling them over.

Fatty longed to get down the tree, go home, and have some supper. He suddenly felt tremendously hungry. He peered down to see if Mr. Tupping had gone. But he hadn't.

He was in the cat-house again, hunting about very carefully. After a while he came out, looking thoughtful, locked the house, and went off up the path still looking thoughtful. Fatty waited till his footsteps had died away, then slithered down the tree.

"Well, we'll see old Luke tomorrow and ask him no end of questions," thought Fatty as he went home. "My word – this has been an exciting day!"

But there were more exciting things to come!

Pip and Bets Pay a Call

Next morning Fatty was down at Pip's house early, longing to tell the others how surprised and puzzled Mr. Goon and the gardener had been when they had found all the "false" clues. Larry and Daisy arrived about the same time as Buster and Fatty, and soon the children were giggling over Fatty's story.

"Clear-Orf asked Tupping if Luke smoked cigars," said Fatty with a chuckle. "I almost fell out of the tree trying not to laugh!"

"We've whistled lots of times to Luke this morning," said Pip, "but he hasn't answered us, or come to the wall either. Do you think he is too frightened to?"

"Perhaps he is," said Fatty. "Well, we simply must talk to him, and tell him about the whistle we found in the cats' cage, and all the clues we put there ourselves. I'll go and whistle awfully loudly."

But not even Fatty's loudest and most vigorous whistling brought any answer. So the children decided to wait at the gate about one o'clock. That was the time when Luke went home to his dinner.

So they waited at the gate. But no Luke appeared. The children waited until ten minutes past one, and then had to rush off to their own meal.

"Perhaps he's got the sack," said Fatty, the idea occurring to him for the first time. "Perhaps he won't come next door any more."

"Oh," said Bets in dismay, "poor Luke! Do you think Lady Candling gave him notice then, and said he wasn't to come any more?"

"How shall we find out?" said Larry.

"We could ask Tupping," said Daisy doubtfully. The others looked at her scornfully.

"As if we'd go and ask Tupping *anything*!" said Larry. They all stood and thought for a moment.

"I know," said Pip. "Lady Candling said I could take Bets in to see her. So I will, this afternoon. And I could ask Lady Candling herself about Luke, couldn't I?"

"Good idea, Pip," said Fatty. "I was just thinking the same thing myself. And also you could take the chance of finding out where Lady Candling was between four and five o'clock perhaps. I mean, find out whether she had any chance of slipping off down to the cats herself, to steal her own Dark Queen away."

"Well, I'm sure she didn't," said Pip at once. "You've only got to look at her to know she couldn't even *think* of doing such a thing! Anyway, I thought we had decided that it wasn't worth while questioning our Suspects, seeing that Luke was by the cat-house all the time during that hour and would have seen anyone there."

"Well, I suppose it isn't really," said Fatty. "I don't see that it's any way possible for the thief to have stolen the cat right under old Luke's nose. He said that he hadn't left the spot for even half a minute."

"There's our dinner-bell *again*," said Bets. "Come on, Pip, we shall get into an awful row. Come back afterwards, you others, and we'll tell you how Pip and I get on this afternoon."

At half-past three Pip and Bets thought they would go and see Lady Candling.

"I think it would be more polite to Lady Candling if you went looking clean," said Daisy. So poor Pip and Bets went into the house to wash and put on clean clothes.

Soon they were walking sedately down the drive, out of the gate, and up Lady Candling's drive. They passed Tupping on the way. He was cutting the hedges there. He scowled at them as they passed.

"Good afternoon, Tupping, what a beautiful day it is!" said Pip, in an imitation of his mother's politeness. "I really think we shall have a little rain before long, though, don't you? Still, the vegetable garden needs it, I'm sure!"

Tupping gave a growl, and snipped viciously at the hedge. Pip felt sure he would like to have snipped at him and Bets. He grinned and went on his way.

The two children went to the front door and rang the bell. A trim little maid came to the door and smiled at the children.

"Please, is Lady Candling in?" asked Pip.

"I think she's in the garden," said the maid. "I'll take you out to the verandah, and you can go and look for her if you like. She may be picking roses."

"Have they found the cat yet?" asked Pip as he and Bets followed the maid out to a sunny verandah.

"No," said the maid. "Miss Harmer's in a great state about her. It's a funny business, isn't it? I'm afraid it must have been Luke. After all, he was the only one near the cats between four and five o'clock."

"Didn't you hear or see anyone strange at all yesterday afternoon?" asked Pip, thinking that he might as well ask a few questions.

"Nobody," said the maid. "You see, Lady Candling had quite a tea-party yesterday – nine or ten people altogether – and Cook and I were busy all the time. We didn't go

61

down the garden at all between four and five o'clock, we had such a lot to do. If we *had* slipped down, we might have seen the thief at his work. Ah! it was a good day for the thief – with Miss Harmer out, and Tupping out, and Cook and me busy, and Lady Candling up here at the house with her friends!"

"It was," said Pip. "It looks as if the thief must have known all that too, to arrange his theft so neatly."

"That's why we think it must be Luke," said the girl. "Though I always liked Luke. A bit simple, but always very kind. And that Tupping's a perfect horror to him."

"Don't you like Tupping either?" said Bets eagerly.

"He's a rude, bad-tempered old man!" said the girl. "But don't you say I said so. Cook and me wish it had been *him* that took the cat. Well, I mustn't talk to you any more. You go out and find her ladyship."

Pip and Bets went into the sunny garden. "From what the maid says it's quite clear that we can cross Lady Candling, the parlourmaid, and the cook off our list of Suspects," said Pip. "Hallo! there's Miss Trimble."

Miss Trimble advanced to meet them. Bets spoke to Pip in a whisper.

"Pip! Let's count how many times her glasses fall off! They keep on doing it."

"Well, children!" said Miss Trimble in her bird-like voice, giving them a wide and toothy smile. "Are you looking for Lady Candling? I think I have seen this little girl before, haven't I? Aren't you the little girl that the strawberry runners ran away with? Oh, what a joke, ha, ha!"

She laughed, and her glasses fell off, dangling on their little chain. She put them on again.

"Yes, I'm the little girl," said Bets. "And we *have* come to see Lady Candling."

"Oh, what a pity! She's just gone out!" said Miss Trimble. "I'm afraid you'll have to put up with poor old me!"

She laughed again, and her glasses fell off. "Twice," said Bets, under her breath.

"Do you know where Luke is?" said Pip, thinking it would be a good idea to go and find him if he was anywhere about.

"No, I don't," said Miss Trimble. "He didn't turn up today. Tupping was very annoyed about it."

"Did Lady Candling give Luke the sack, Miss Tremble?" asked Bets.

"My name is Trimble, not Tremble," said Miss Trimble.

"No, Lady Candling didn't give him notice. At least, I don't think so. Wasn't it a pity about that lovely cat? I saw her at four o'clock, you know."

"Yes, you were with my mother," said Pip. "I suppose you didn't see anyone near the cat-house except Luke?"

"No, nobody," said Miss Trimble. "Luke was there, of course, digging hard all the time. Your mother and I were only there a minute or two, then I had to hurry back to the tea-table, because there was a lot for me to do there. I didn't have a moment to myself until after the party."

"Then *you* couldn't have stolen the cat!" said Pip, with a laugh. Miss Trimble jumped, and her glasses fell off. Her nose went even redder than it already was.

"What a funny joke!" she said, and she tried to disentangle her glasses from her lace collar. "The very idea of stealing *anything* makes me go hot and cold!"

"Could we go and see the cats, Miss Tremble?" asked Bets.

"I should think so," said Miss Trimble. "My name is Trimble, not Tremble. Do try and remember. Miss Harmer is with the cats. We'll go and see her. Come along, dears."

She tripped along in front of them, her glasses on her nose once more. They fell off going down a few steps, and Bets counted out loud.

"That's four times."

"Four times what, dear?" said Miss Trimble, turning round and smiling sweetly. She put up her hand to stop her glasses from falling.

"Don't stop them," said Bets. "I'm counting how many times they fall off."

"Oh, what a funny little girl!" said Miss Trimble, looking rather cross. She held her glasses on with her hand, and Bets was sorry. She felt that wasn't fair!

They came to the cat-house. Miss Harmer was there, mixing some food. She looked up. Her plump, jolly face looked worried.

"Hallo!" she said. "Come to see my cats?"

"Yes, please," said Bets. "Miss Harmer, wasn't it awful Dark Queen being stolen whilst you were away?"

"Yes," said the kennel-girl, stirring the food in the pan. "I wish I hadn't gone. I should only have taken half a day, really; but Mr. Tupping offered to look after the cats for me if I'd like the whole day – so I thanked him and went. But I've reproached myself ever since."

"Mr. *Tupping* offered to look after the cats, did you say?" said Pip, full of amazement at the thought of Tupping offering to do anyone a kindness. "Golly! that's not like *him*."

"No, it isn't," said the girl, with a laugh. "But I badly wanted to go home, and I can't unless I have a whole day, because my home is so far away. Do you collect railway tickets? Because the collector didn't take my ticket when I got back to the station last night. You can have it if you like."

Pip did collect railway tickets. He took the return-half that Miss Harmer held out to him. "Thanks," he said, "I'd like it." He put it into his pocket, thinking how envious Larry would be, for he collected railway tickets too.

"Do you think Luke stole the cat, Miss Harmer?" said Pip.

"No, I don't," said Miss Harmer. "He's a bit silly, but he's honest enough. But I tell you who *might* have taken the cat – that circus friend of Luke's! What's his name now – Jake, I think it is."

This was news to the two children. Luke had never told them about Jake. A circus friend! How exciting! Why had Luke never mentioned him?

"Does Jake live near here?" asked Pip.

"Oh no, but the circus he belongs to is performing in the next town – in Farring," said Miss Harmer. "So I suppose he's somewhere near. You know, Dark Queen would be marvellous in a circus. I had already taught her to do a few tricks."

Miss Trimble was getting impatient, for it was near her tea-time. She gave three or four polite little coughs, and her glasses promptly fell off.

"We'd better go," said Pip. "Thanks for showing us the cats. You needn't bother to show us out, Miss Tremble. We'll go over the wall."

"My name is Trimble, not Tremble," said Miss Trimble, losing her smile for a moment. "I wish you would try and remember. And surely you should not go over the wall? Let me take you down the drive."

"Tupping's there," said Bets. Miss Trimble's glasses fell off at once at the mention of the surly gardener.

"Oh well, if you *really* want to get over the wall, I won't stop you!" she said. "Good-bye, dear children. I'll tell Lady Candling you came."

"They fell off eight times," said Bets in a pleased tone as the two of them climbed over the wall. "I say, Pip, isn't it funny that Luke never told us about Jake?"

A Visit to the Circus

Pip and Bets were to go to tea with Larry and Daisy that afternoon, so they all went up the lane together, Fatty and Buster too. Pip had a lot to tell.

"Luke hasn't turned up today," he said. "It's funny, isn't it, because Lady Candling hasn't given him notice. And I say, I wonder why he never told us about Jake."

"I suppose – I suppose he couldn't possibly have told Jake to come to the cat-house yesterday, and he couldn't possibly have given *him* the cat, could he?" said Larry.

"I mean – I know we think Luke didn't do it – but, well, what do you others think?"

For the first time a small doubt about Luke came into the children's minds. He hadn't told them about Jake. And he was a man they would have liked to hear about if he lived with a circus. And after all, Luke had been the only one near the cat-house during the whole of that hour.

"Well, I still don't believe it was Luke or his friend Jake," said Bets stoutly. "So there!"

"Nor do I," said Daisy. "But I wish everything wasn't so dreadfully puzzling."

"We were much better find-outers last time," said Larry gloomily. "Think of the clues and things we found, and all the Suspects we questioned."

"Well," said Pip, "I can tell you this – all the Suspects on our list can be crossed off now. I was only about half an hour in next door, but I found out enough to know that not one of the people on our list could have stolen Dark Queen."

"How do you know?" asked Fatty.

"Well, Lady Candling had quite a big party," said Pip, "and it stands to reason she couldn't leave a big party and go off to steal her own cat in the middle of it. The cook and parlourmaid were very busy all the time during the tea-hour, so that rules them out too. Miss Tremble had to help as well, and I'm sure Lady Candling would have been very suspicious if she'd gone off for ten minutes or so to steal the cat!"

"Go on, Pip," said Fatty. "Where's your list of Suspects, Larry? Let's cross them off one by one."

"And you can cross off Miss Harmer," said Pip, "because she went home yesterday and her home is at Langston, miles away. And look, here's the return-half she gave me, because the collector didn't take it when she got back. So we can cross her off too."

"That's all the Suspects crossed off – except Luke," said Larry. "Golly! it does look as if it might have been a friend of Luke's, doesn't it – someone who came slipping up, winked at Luke, took the cat and went off, trusting to Luke not to give him away. I wish we could find Luke and question him about Jake."

"I know where Luke is – I bet I know!" said Pip. "I bet he's gone to the circus – and he's with his friend Jake! I'll bet he'll go off with the circus, too, when it moves away!"

Everyone felt certain that Pip was right. Of course that was where Luke would be.

"Look here, let's get out our bikes after tea and ride over to Farring," said Fatty. "We'll soon find the circus-tents, and if Luke's there we'll find him too!"

"Good idea!" said everyone, brightening up at the thought of doing something exciting. "Come on, let's hurry up over tea and go."

Mrs. Daykin (Larry's mother and Daisy's) was astonished to find the children galloping so fast through the lovely tea she had provided for them. She looked at them in astonishment.

"Are you terribly hungry, or just in a hurry?" she asked. "Didn't any of you have any dinner?"

"We're just in a hurry, Mrs. Daykin, that's all," said Fatty, as politely as he could with his mouth full. "We want to go for a bike-ride after tea."

"To Farring," put in Bets. She got two hard nudges at once, one from Pip and one from Larry. They were both afraid she would say too much.

"Why to Farring?" said Mrs. Daykin, surprised. She didn't know the circus was there. "It's not a very pretty place."

"Well, we thought it would be quite a nice ride there and back," said Larry. "We'd better be going now. We'll not be late home, Mother."

Fatty had to go and get his bicycle, and so had Bets and Pip. To her joy Bets was allowed to come, as Farring was not a great distance away. The children rode off gaily.

Soon, in front of them, they saw another bicyclist — a big burly one, dressed in dark blue.

"Golly! There's old Clear-Orf!" said Pip. "Don't catch him up, anyone. He may turn off somewhere, and then we can get on quickly on our way to Farring."

But Clear-orf took the way to Farring too! "I say! I hope he isn't going to see Jake as well," said Fatty in dismay. "Do you suppose he got out of Luke that he had a circus friend? Blow! We can't let Clear-Orf get ahead of us like this. After all, Jake may be a fine big Clue."

Then a lovely thing happened. Mr. Goon got a puncture! He rode over a piece of glass, and his back tyre went flat quite suddenly. The big policeman bumped along the road, gave a loud and angry exclamation, and got off.

He took his bike to the side of the road and got out a puncture-mending outfit. The children, grinning, rode quickly by. Fatty waved to him.

"Evening, Mr. Goon! Sorry to see you are in trouble!"

The policeman looked up in surprise that turned to annoyance when he saw the five children cycling quickly on the way to Farring. He began to mend his inner tube. The children simply sped along, knowing that they had at least a quarter of an hour before Clear-Orf could catch them up.

"There's the circus-tents," said Bets, as they topped a hill and rode down. "And look at the cages, too — and the gay caravans. Oh, I do think it looks exciting!"

It was exciting. A big elephant was tethered by a hind leg to a stout tree. Five tigers in a very strong cage roared for their dinner. Seven beautiful black horses were being ridden round the field by the grooms, who were giving them a little exercise.

Smoke rose from the chimneys of the gay caravans, and all kinds of exciting smells rose on the air.

"What's our plan?" said Larry, jumping off his bicycle and leaning it against the fence. "Do we hunt round for Luke, or do we ask for Jake?"

"We'll all go, except Bets," said Larry. "It can't matter us wandering separately round the field. I can see other children doing it too. But Bets had better stay and look after the bikes."

The others climbed over the fence and went in to the field. They separated and wandered about, waiting to meet someone they could ask about Jake.

It was Pip who found Jake. He had asked a cheeky little circus-girl if she knew where Jake was, and she had first put out her tongue at him, then called him an impolite name, and then pointed to where a big man was giving a pail of water to a horse.

Pip went across to him. The man looked up. "What do you want?" he said.

"I say," said Pip, "I'm looking for a boy I know, called Luke. I've got a message for him. Is he here?"

"Nope," said the man shortly. "Haven't seen him for weeks."

Pip was disappointed. "Oh," he said. "I did want to talk to him. You don't know his address, do you?"

"Nope," said the man again. "I don't give addresses to little busybodies. You go away and mind your own business."

Fatty came up when he saw Pip talking to the man. "Is this Jake?" he said to Pip. Pip nodded.

"But he says he hasn't seen Luke for weeks," said Pip.

"We're his friends," said Fatty earnestly. "Please believe us. We just want to talk to him."

"I've told you I don't know where he is," said the man.

"Now you get out of this field; and just remember what I say, I haven't seen Luke for weeks."

Bets stood by the bicycles, watching the others wandering about the camp. She kept an eye open for old Clear-Orf, and hoped he wouldn't stop and ask her what she was doing there if he came by. She decided to creep through to the other side of the hedge, where she would be hidden from any passer-by.

So she crept through and settled herself comfortably there. She was near a bright-red caravan. She looked up at it, and saw something that gave her an enormous surprise. Somebody was peeping at her from behind the little lace curtain – and that somebody was Luke!

Luke Again

Bets sat quite still, holding her breath. The curtain was then drawn a little farther, and the window was quietly opened. Luke put his head out.

"Hallo, little Bets!" he said in a cautious voice. "Why are you here? Have you come to see the circus?"

"No," said Bets, standing up and speaking in a low voice too. "We heard you had a friend here, Luke, and we wanted to find you and talk to you – so we thought perhaps you had gone to your friend."

"He's my uncle," said Luke. "I don't like him much, but I couldn't think of anyone else to go to. You see, I was afraid they'd put me into prison for stealing Dark Queen. So I ran away."

"But you didn't steal her, did you?" said Bets.

"'Course not," said Luke. "As if I'd go stealing anything! I'd be too scared, let alone it's wrong. Are you alone?"

"No; the others are here too," said Bets. "They have gone to find Jake to ask if you are here."

"Oh," said Luke. "Well, I didn't tell him anything about the trouble I'm in – nothing about Dark Queen, I mean. I was afraid if I told him that he'd not hide me here. I just told him I'd got into trouble with my stepfather and wanted to run away with the circus. I showed him the bruises where my stepfather hit me last night, and he said he'd hide me till the circus went away and take me with him. He can do with a strong lad like me to help."

"Did your stepfather beat you?" said Bets, with great sympathy. "Oh, Luke, you do have a bad time, don't you? I hope the others don't say anything to Jake about the stolen cat; but I don't think they will. They were only going to say that they wanted to give you a message."

"Well, if they tell him I'm suspected of stealing anything, he'll not keep me here, that's certain," said Luke. "No circus-folk like to be mixed up with the police. Don't you go and tell anyone I'm here, will you, Bets? I've got to keep hidden in this caravan till the circus moves off."

"I won't tell a soul – except the boys and Daisy," said Bets. "You can depend on that."

"Oh, and Luke – I must tell you something queer," said Bets, remembering the finding of the whistle. But before she could say any more, there came the sound of voices nearby. Luke shut the window hastily, and drew the curtain.

It was only the boys and Daisy coming back to Bets, bitterly disappointed.

"Nothing doing, Bets," said Fatty. "We found Jake, and he wouldn't open his mouth about Luke at all. Said he hadn't seen him for weeks."

"But all the same I can't help feeling that he *has* seen him and that he knows where he is," said Pip. "It's sickening – coming all this way for nothing."

"What's the matter with Bets?" said Fatty, looking at her suddenly. "She's all red, and bursting to tell us something. What's up, Bets?"

"Nothing," said Bets. "Except that I know where Luke is, that's all."

The four children stared at Bets as if she had suddenly gone mad. "What do you mean?" said Pip at last. "Where is he?"

Bets dropped her voice. "See that red caravan over there? Well – he's hiding in there. I saw him. He was peeping out at me. And I talked to him."

"Did you say anything to Jake about the stolen cat?" continued Bets. "Because Luke said he didn't say a word to him about that in case Jake wouldn't hide him. He just told Jake that he was running away from his stepfather, and he showed him his bruises."

"We didn't say a word about the cat, silly, of course not," said Pip. "I wonder if we can speak to Luke. Which window did he look out of, did you say?"

Bets showed him. Pip whistled the little tune that Luke always used as a signal. The curtain moved slightly, and the children could see the outline of Luke's head behind. The window softly opened.

"Hallo there, Luke!" said Fatty in a low voice. "We haven't said anything to Jake about the cat. I say, are you really running away with the circus?"

"Yes," said Luke.

"But don't you think that everyone will feel certain you stole Dark Queen if you run away?" said Larry. "You know, it's not a very good plan to run away from things."

There came the sound of somebody jumping off a bicycle the other side of the hedge – somebody heavy and panting. The children looked at one another, and then looked over the hedge. Yes, just as they had feared – it was Mr. Goon. His puncture was mended and he had caught them up.

"These your bikes?" said Mr. Goon. "What you doing here?"

"Having a look round the circus," said Fatty politely. "Lovely tigers here, Mr. Goon. You'll have to be careful they don't eat you. They like a nice big dinner."

Mr. Goon snorted. "You'd better clear orf," he said. "You're up to no good here, I'll be bound. Have you seen your friend Luke?"

"Luke?" said Fatty, staring with wide eyes at Mr. Goon. "Why, where *is* Luke? Isn't he at Lady Candling's? We'd like to talk to him, if only you'll tell us where he is."

"You clear orf," said Mr. Goon again, getting on his bicycle. "Butting in where you're not wanted. Interfering with the Law."

He rode off to the gate that led into the field. The children did not dare to speak to Luke again. They slipped through the hedge and got their bikes. They saw Mr. Goon speak to someone and then go off to where Jake was still watering his horses.

"There, just what we thought!" said Fatty. "He's heard about Jake too. I only hope Jake won't give away Luke's hiding-place when he knows he's suspected of stealing Dark Queen!"

"We'd better get away from this caravan," said Pip. "It might look funny, being so near it. Old Clear-Orf is terribly stupid, but it might occur to him that we are interested in this caravan for some special reason!"

So they all rode off, leaving poor Luke behind in the red caravan. How they wished they could do something for him. But they couldn't. They must just hope he could get away safely with Jake and that nobody would find him.

"All the same, I think he's jumped out of the frying-pan into the fire," said Larry as they cycled home together. "I don't think he's going to be any happier with that surly Jake than with Tupping or his stepfather."

It was late when they got back, almost Bets' bed-time. "We'd better say good night," said Larry, stopping at the corner of the road where he lived. "See you all tomorrow!"

"Good night," called the others, and rode on, leaving Daisy and Larry behind.

"We'll drop you next, Fatty," said Pip.

"Good-bye," said Bets, "see you tomorrow." She and Pip rode home down the lane. Bets' bed-time bell was ringing as she rode up the drive.

"Just in time," said Pip. "You won't get into a row to-night, that's certain! Happy dreams, Bets!"

He soon fell asleep. He dreamt all kinds of things. He dreamt that old Clear-Orf was chasing him, riding on Buster's back. He dreamt that Jake joined in, riding on a tiger. Then he dreamt that Luke was in front of them, running away in fright. He heard the tuneful whistle that Luke used as a signal.

Pip turned in his sleep. The dream went on. Luke was in it all the time. The whistle kept there too, insistent and clear.

Then someone clutched Pip, and he awoke with a terrible jump. He sat up, trembling, still thinking of his dream. He gave a little yelp.

"Sh! It's me, Pip," said Bets' voice. "Don't make a noise."

"Bets!" said Pip in anger. "What do you mean by giving me a fright like this? You nearly made me jump out of my skin."

"Pip, listen! There's someone whistling in the garden," whispered Bets. "And it's Luke's little tune. You know, the one we always used to whistle to one another. Do you think it's Luke out there? Does he want us?"

Pip was now wide awake. He was just about to answer Bets when he heard the whistle again, the noise he had heard in his dreams. He now knew it had been a real whistle, not a dream one. He jumped out of bed.

"Good for you, Bets!" he said. "It must be Luke. He's left the circus for some reason and come back here. We'd better see what he wants. At least – I'll go and see what he wants. You stay here."

"I'm coming too," said Bets in an obstinate voice. "I heard him, and you didn't. I'm coming too."

"You'll only fall down the stairs or something and make a row," said Pip.

"I shan't," said Bets crossly, raising her voice. Pip nudged her.

"Shut up! You'll wake everyone. All right – come if you want to, but for goodness' sake be quiet."

They did not bother to put on dressing-gowns, for the night was so warm. They padded down the passage and on to the landing. Pip fell over something, and rolled down a few stairs before he was able to catch hold of the banisters and stop himself from falling any farther.

"What's the matter, Pip?" said Bets in alarm.

"Fell over the silly kitchen cat," whispered back Pip. "Golly, I hope no one heard me."

The two sat on the stairs holding their breath for a minute or two, expecting to hear a movement in their parents' room. But nobody stirred. The cat sat at the bottom of the stairs, her green eyes gleaming in the darkness.

"I believe she tripped me up on purpose," said Pip. "She's been awful cross ever since we let Buster into the house. Get away, Puss."

The cat mewed and fled. The children went groping their way down the dark passage to the garden door. Pip unlocked it, and they stepped out into the silent garden. Bets clung to Pip's hand. She didn't very much like the dark.

The whistle sounded again. "It's somewhere at the top of the garden," said Pip. "Come on! Keep on the grass, Bets. The gravel makes a noise."

The two crept over the lawn, up the kitchen-garden, and round past the big rubbish-heap. A shadow moved by the old summer-house.

It was Luke! They heard his voice in the darkness. So Luke had come back after all!

Luke Finds Some Good Friends

"Luke! Is that you?" whispered Pip. "What's the matter? Why did you leave the circus?"

Pip drew Luke into the summer-house. Bets sat on one side of him and Pip on the other. Bets slipped her little hand into Luke's big rough paw. The big boy held it there gently.

"Yes. I left the circus camp," he said. "That policeman went to my Uncle Jake, and he told him all about the stolen cat and that he thought I'd taken it – and he said did my uncle know anything about the cat."

"And I suppose your uncle sent you off when he heard all that," said Pip.

"He didn't give me away to the policeman," said Luke. "He said he hadn't heard of no stolen cat, and he hadn't seen me for weeks and didn't want to. I reckon a search will be made of the circus, though, because that bobby is quite certain Dark Queen is somewhere there."

"I suppose they'd make a search for you too," said Bets.

"Yes," said Luke. "Well, my uncle waited till the bobby was safely out of sight, then he came to me and told me to go. Said he didn't mind me running away from my step-father, but he wasn't going to help me run away from the police."

"But you can't go back to your stepfather!" said Pip. "He's awful to you."

"'Course I can't," said Luke. "Don't want to be half killed, do I? Thing is – what am I going to do? I came here tonight because I thought you might be able to give me something to eat. I've had nothing since twelve o'clock and I'm fair starved."

"Oh, *poor* Luke!" said Bets. "I'll go and get you something at once. There's a steak-pie in the larder and a plum-tart. I saw them both."

"Here, Bets, don't be an idiot," said Pip, pulling her back. "What do you suppose Mother will say in the morning if she finds both pie and tart gone? You can't tell a lie and say you don't know anything about it. Then, if you have to own up, people will ask you whom you gave the stuff to and they'll guess it's Luke."

"Well, what shall we give him then?" asked Bets.

"Bread and butter," said Pip. "That won't be missed. And we could take a small bun or two out of the tin. And there's lots of plums and greengages."

"That'll do fine," said Luke gratefully. Bets sped off at once to the kitchen. Soon she had collected the food and was back with Luke and Pip. Luke began to munch hungrily.

"I'm feeling better now," he said. "Nothing like hunger to make you feel miserable, I always say."

"Where are you going to sleep tonight?" asked Pip.

"Don't know," said Luke. "Under a hedge somewhere. Reckon I'd better go tramping."

"Don't do that," said Bets. "You stay with us for a little while. You can sleep in this old summer-house. We can put the mattress from the swing-seat on the bench here and you can sleep on that."

"And we'll bring you food each day till we think of some plan for you," said Pip, feeling rather excited. "It will be fun."

"I don't want to get you into no trouble," said Luke.

"Well, Luke, you won't," said Pip. "You stay in our garden, and maybe we'll be able to solve the mystery of Dark Queen, and then you can go back to your job and everything will be all right."

"I'll get the mattress off the swing-seat now," said Bets, and she ran to get it in the dark. She was more used to the dark now, and she found the swing-seat without difficulty. Pip went to help her. Together the two dragged the mattress up the garden to where Luke sat in the summer-house.

They made a bed on the bench with the mattress and then Pip fetched an old rug from the garage.

"It's a warm night," he said to Luke. "You won't be too cold. We'll bring you some breakfast tomorrow morning."

"What about your gardener?" said Luke fearfully. "What time does he come? Will he be up here at all?"

"He's ill," said Pip. "He won't be back for a few days. Mother's fed up because of the vegetables. She says they want weeding, and she keeps on trying to make me and Bets do it. But I hate weeding."

"Oh," said Luke, relieved. "Well, I'll be pretty safe up here then. Good night – and thanks."

It was exciting to wake the next morning and think of Luke in the summer-house. Pip sat up in bed and wondered what there was for breakfast. It it was sausages he could secrete one somehow and take it to Luke. If it was boiled eggs he couldn't. Anyway, he could take bread and butter.

Bets was thinking the same thing. She dressed quickly and went downstairs, wondering if she could cut some bread and butter before anyone came into the dining-room. She thought she could.

But just as she was cutting a big thick slice of bread, her mother came in. She stared in surprise at Bets.

"Whatever are you doing?" she said. "Are you so hungry that you can't wait for breakfast? And what an enormously thick slice, Bets!"

Poor Bets had to put the slice on her own plate and eat it. The porridge was brought in and she and Pip ate theirs. Then – hurrah! – a dish of sausages came in! The children's eyes gleamed. Now they would be able to take one or two to Luke.

"Please can I have two sausages today?" asked Pip.

"Me too," said Bets.

"Gracious, you must be hungry, Bets!" said her mother. She gave them each two. Their father was hidden

Luke sat in the summerhouse, eating

behind his newspaper, so he would not be able to see what they were doing. But their mother could see quite well. How could they manage to hide away a sausage each? It was going to be difficult.

But just then Annie the maid came into the room. "Would you care to buy a flag for our local hospital, Madam?" she said. "Miss Lacy is at the front door."

"Oh, of course," said Mrs. Hilton, and got up to get her bag, which she had left upstairs. The two children winked at one another. Pip got out a clean hanky and wrapped a sausage up quickly. Bets did the same – but her hanky was not so clean! They pushed the wrapped-up sausages into their pockets with slices of bread, just as their mother came back.

Luke was glad of the bread and sausages. They took him some water to drink too. He sat in the summer-house eating, and they talked in low voices. "We'll bring you something at dinner-time too," said Pip. "And you can pick yourself plums and greengages from the trees, can't you, Luke?"

Luke nodded. He drank the water and handed back the cup. Then there came the sound of someone calling "Coee" and Bets jumped up.

"It's Fatty – and Buster! Hie, Fatty, here we are in the summer-house."

Fatty came up the garden with Buster. The little Scottie darted into the summer-house, barking with delight to see his friend there. Luke patted him.

Fatty stopped at the entrance to the summer-house, his mouth falling open in the greatest amazement when he saw Luke there. Bets laughed at his surprise.

"We're going to hide him here," she explained to Fatty. "And we're going to bring him food. It's exciting. Oh, Fatty, can't we solve the mystery so that Luke isn't afraid any more? Do let's hurry up and solve the mystery! "

Fatty had to hear all about the night's happenings. Then Daisy and Larry came, and added their surprise and delight to the little company. Altogether it was a very pleasant morning.

"Where's that whistle we found in the cats' cage?" said Pip. It was produced and held up for Luke to see.

"We found it in the cage," said Fatty. "And as we thought Mr. Goon would be sure to find it, and Mr. Tupping would tell him it was yours, we took it out and kept it. And we put a lot of false clues in the cage. You'd have laughed to see them. I put a cigar-end in the cage and one under it!"

Luke whistled. "Oho!" he said, "so that's why Mr. Goon got all excited when he found my uncle smoking a cigar! I couldn't think why he did. My uncle said he went quite purple in the face when he took out a cigar and lighted it. He had a box given to him once, and when he wants to be careful what he says to anyone, he lights one of those cigars and smokes it. He says it helps him to think."

The children giggled to think that Fatty's cigar-ends had made Mr. Goon get all excited when he saw Jake smoking a cigar. Then Luke looked at the whistle that Fatty held.

"Yes; that's one I made," he said. "I lost it somewhere in the garden. How could it have got into the cats' cage? I made that whistle months ago."

They all talked over the mystery again, but somehow they could not make head or tail of it.

Between them the children managed to supply Luke with plenty of food. They gave him a pail of water and soap and an old towel. They made up a bed for him each night in the summer-house. And, in return, Luke worked in the vegetable garden whenever Pip's mother was out, weeding it carefully and doing all he could to make it nice. The kitchen-garden was far away from the house and he could not be seen.

"Must do something in return for your kindness," he said to the children. And they liked him all the better for it. For three days Luke stayed in Pip's garden, and then things began to happen again.

Mr. Goon is Very Suspicious

One afternoon Mr. Goon met Fatty and Buster, and he stopped them.

"I want a word with you, Master Frederick," he said in his pompous voice.

"I'm afraid I can't stop," said Fatty in a polite voice. "I'm taking Buster for a walk."

"You just stop where you are," said Clear-Orf angrily. "I tell you I've got something to say to you."

"Well, what you say to me is usually 'clear orf,' " said Fatty. "Are you sure that isn't what you want to say?"

"Now, look here," said Mr. Goon, coming to the point at last, "I think you and them other children knows where Luke is. See? And I'm just warning you. If you hide him or know where he's hiding and don't inform the police, you'll get into Serious trouble. Very Serious Trouble."

Fatty was startled. Why did Mr. Goon suspect that they knew where Luke was, or were hiding him?

"What makes you think we'd try to hide Luke?" he said. "As if we could hide him without *you* knowing, Mr. Goon! Why a clever policeman like you knows everything!"

"Ah," said Mr. Goon. "I know a lot more than you think."

That apparently was the end of the talk. Mr. Goon shut his notebook with a snap and went on his way. Fatty went down the lane, thinking hard.

"Old Tupping must have popped his head over the wall, and either spotted Luke or thought he did," thought Fatty. "Blow! We don't want to get into trouble. But what are we to do with poor old Luke? Perhaps we had better give him some money and get him away."

The others listened to what Fatty told them. Bets was upset. "Don't send Luke away," she said. "We might solve the mystery any time, and then he could go back to Lady Candling's."

"We shan't solve this mystery," said Fatty gloomily. "We aren't so clever as we thought we were. I bet even Inspector Jenks wouldn't be able to solve the mystery of Dark Queen."

"Oooh!" said Daisy at once, remembering how nice and friendly the Inspector had been in the Easter holidays when they had solved another mystery. "Inspector Jenks! I'd forgotten about him. Can't we get into touch with him and tell him about poor old Luke? I'm sure he wouldn't want to put him into prison or anything. He'd keep our secret all right."

"Do you think he would?" said Larry. "Well, I'm blessed if I can see any way out of this. If old Clear-Orf starts searching Pip's garden he'll find Luke, and then maybe it will be worse for him, and bad for us. Let's tell the Inspector. He always said he would help us and be a friend to us if he could."

"I'll telephone," said Fatty. The others looked at him respectfully. They thought it was rather marvellous of Fatty to offer to telephone to what Bets called "A very, very high-up policeman."

Fatty kept his word. He went back home, waited until no one was about to hear him, and then put a call through to the police-station in the nearest big town, where the Inspector lived.

Very luckily for him, Inspector Jenks happened to be there. He came to the telephone and spoke pleasantly to Fatty.

"Ah, Master Frederick Trotteville? I hope you are well. Yes, yes; I well remember the most interesting time we had together in the Easter holidays, when you so kindly solved the mystery of the burnt cottage – very clever piece of work, if I may say so. And have you solved any other mysteries since?"

"Well, sir, there *is* a mystery here we can't solve," said Fatty, relieved to find the Inspector so very friendly. "We simply can't. I don't know if you've heard of it. A very valuable cat disappeared."

The Inspector appeared to think hard for a minute. Then his voice came again over the phone.

"Yes; the report came in to me. I remember it. I believe our friend Mr. Goon is in charge of that particular puzzle."

"Well, he isn't exactly a friend of *ours*," said Fatty honestly. "But the person who is supposed to have done the crime *is* a friend of ours. And that's what I'm really ringing up about. We're in a bit of a muddle about him. I was just wondering if by any chance you could give us a little advice."

"Very nice of you to ask me," said the Inspector. "It so happens I am coming through your village tomorrow. I suppose you couldn't invite me to tea – say a picnic tea by the river?"

"Oh, *yes*," said Fatty joyfully. "That would be simply fine. We could tell you everything then."

"Then that's settled," said the Inspector. "I'll be along your lane about four o'clock. It will be most pleasant for us all to meet again. I hope you agree with me."

"Oh, I do," said Fatty. "Good-bye, sir, and thank you very much."

Fatty put down the receiver and sped down the lane to Pip's house, full of excitement. He ran up the drive and found the others in the garden.

"Well," said Fatty, "that's all settled. The Inspector is coming to tea with us tomorrow – a picnic tea down by the river. We'll tell him everything."

"Fatty! Is he really coming? Did you ask him to tea? Oh, Fatty, how marvellous!" cried the others. Fatty swelled up, full of pride and importance.

"You want a fellow like me to arrange these things," he said. "It's nothing to me to get things like this done. You'd better leave everything to me."

"Shut up!" said Larry and Pip at once. But they could not be annoyed with Fatty's boasting for long, because they were all so excited at the thought of seeing the big, kindly Inspector once more. Bets was really thrilled. She had liked him so much, and he had put everything right at once last time. Perhaps he could this time.

"We'll plan a fine tea," said Daisy. "We'll tell our mothers who is coming with us, and they are sure to let us have anything we want. Even grown-ups seem to think that Inspectors are somebody to make a fuss about!"

Daisy was right. As soon as the children's mothers knew that the great Inspector Jenks had condescended to have a picnic tea with the children, they provided a very fine meal.

The children packed up the food, and went to stand at the front gate to watch for the Inspector. Mr. Goon came riding down on his bicycle. He jumped off when he saw them.

"I'd like a word with you," he said in his pompous voice.

"Sorry," said Larry, "but we're on our way to a picnic. I bet you'd like to come – it's going to be a gorgeous one."

Mr. Goon looked in astonishment at all the food. "You going to eat all that yourselves?" he said suspiciously. Fatty guessed that he thought they were going to take some to Luke. He grinned.

"Oh, no," said Fatty. "The food is for somebody else besides ourselves, Mr. Goon. We shan't tell you who. That would be giving away a secret."

"Hmmmm!" said Mr. Goon, feeling more and more suspicious. "Where are you going for your picnic?"

"Down by the river," said Bets. Mr. Goon got on his bicycle and rode away, thinking hard. Fatty chuckled.

"He thinks we're taking this food to Luke in some hiding-place somewhere," he said. "He doesn't know we're having a picnic with the Inspector. I say, wouldn't it be perfectly marvellous if he tried to follow us and pounced on us to see if we really had got Luke with us – and all the time it was Inspector Jenks?"

"Yes, marvellous," said Daisy. "Oh, look, here's the Inspector!"

It was. He drove up in a very smart black police car, parked it in Pip's garage, and then shook hands solemnly all round. "Very, very pleased to meet you all again," he said, with his beaming smile.

They all went down the lane to the river, Bets hanging on to his arm. The Inspector was a tall, burly man, with twinkling eyes, a smiling mouth, and a very clever face. He looked very fine indeed in his uniform. Bets chattered to him, telling him all the good things they had got for tea.

"We'll have our meal straight away, shall we?" said the Inspector. "You are making my mouth water. Now, where shall we sit?"

Mr. Goon has a Bad Time

They found a nice sheltered place close to the water. Behind them rose an overhanging bank with trees. No one could see them there. It was a good place to talk.

"Well, now," said the Inspector, when the meal was finished and there was very little left – "Well, now, what about a little business? I've looked up the report of the case you told me about, so I know all the details. But I should very much like to hear what you have to say. You tell me that this boy, Luke, is a friend of yours?"

The children began to talk eagerly, telling Inspector Jenks all that they knew, but they did not tell him about the false clues they had laid for Tupping and Clear-Orf. Nobody quite liked to tell him that.

Then they came to where they had talked to Luke at the circus, and how he had come to them one night.

"And ever since then we've fed Luke and let him sleep in the summer-house," said Pip. "But now we think Clear-Orf – Mr. Goon, I mean – has guessed we're hiding him, and we're afraid if we go on doing it we may get him and ourselves into trouble."

"Very wise of you to come to me," said the Inspector. "Yes; you mustn't hide Luke, that is certain. For one thing it tells against Luke, if he runs away and hides. That is never a good thing to do. But he won't be put into prison, don't be afraid of that. For one thing, he is only fifteen – and for another thing, we don't put people into prison unless it is really proved that they have committed a crime. And it is by no means proved that Luke stole the cat, although I admit that things do look very black against him. I am sure you agree with me?"

"Yes. We think they do too," said Fatty. "It has puzzled us very much. Because, you see, Inspector, we know and like Luke, and we don't see how a boy like him *could* have done such a thing."

"Well, I would advise Luke to come out of hiding and go back to his job," said the Inspector. "Er – I don't see that he need say anything about *where* he has been, or *who* has hidden him. No need for that at all."

"He'll have to go back to his stepfather," said Bets, "and oh, Inspector Jenks, he's got such a *cruel* stepfather. He'll beat him."

"No, he won't," said the Inspector. "I shall have a word with him. I think you'll find that he'll let Luke severely alone. In the meantime, I will look more carefully into this mystery and see if I can get a little light shed on it. It certainly sounds most interesting now that I have heard all you have told me."

"What's up with Buster?" said Fatty at that moment.

Buster had left the little company and could be heard barking madly at the top of the bank. Then a voice came to their ears.

"Call this dog orf! Get him under control, or I'll report him!"

"It's old Clear-Orf!" whispered Daisy gleefully. "He's tracked us after all! I bet he thinks we've got Luke down here! Old Buster must have heard him creeping up and gone and barked at him!"

Fatty went up the bank and through the overhanging bushes, and stood on the top, looking at a very angry Mr. Goon.

"Ho! I knew you were down there," said Mr. Goon. "Yes, and I know who you've got with you too!"

"Then I wonder you're not a bit more polite about it," said Fatty in a smooth voice.

"Polite about it! Why should I be?" said Mr. Goon. "Ah, I've caught you properly, I have – harbouring someone who's done a crime! You've gone too far this time, you have. You call this dog orf, and let me go down the bank and get my hands on you-know-who."

Fatty gave a chuckle. He called Buster off and held him by the collar, standing politely aside whilst Mr. Goon pushed his way through the bushes, and then jumped down beside the water, expecting to find four frightened children and a very scared Luke.

Instead, to his awful horror and amazement, he found his Inspector! Mr. Goon simply could not believe his eyes. They always bulged out, but now they looked as if they were going to drop out. He stood and stared at Inspector Jenks and could not utter a word.

"Good afternoon, Goon," said the Inspector.

"G-g-g-g-g-g," began Goon, and then swallowed hastily. "G-g-g-g-good afternoon, sir, I d-d-d-didn't expect to see you here."

"I thought I heard you say you wanted to get your hands on me," said the Inspector. Goon swallowed hard again, loosened his collar with his finger, and then tried to smile.

"You will have your joke, sir," he said in a rather trembling voice. "I – er – I – expected to find somebody else. It's – it's a great surprise to see you here, sir."

"Well, these children have paid me the honour of consulting me about this little affair of the stolen cat," said the Inspector. "Sit down, Goon. It would be good to hear your version of the business. I suppose you haven't got very far with the case?"

"Well, sir – I've got a lot of clues, sir," said Mr. Goon eagerly, hoping to alter the Inspector's opinion of him. "I'd like your advice on them, sir, now you're here, sir."

He took a white envelope from his pocket and opened it. Out came the two cigar-ends, the blue button, the half hair-ribbon, the peppermint drop, and the brown shoe-lace. The Inspector stared at them in considerable astonishment.

"Are all these clues?" he asked at last.

"Yes, sir," said Goon. "Found in the place where the crime was committed, sir. In the cat-house itself."

"Did you *really* find all these things in the cat-house?" said the Inspector, looking at everything as if he really could not believe they were there. "Was this peppermint drop there, Goon?"

"Yes, sir, everything. Never found so many clues in my life before, sir," said Goon, pleased to see the Inspector's surprise.

"Neither have I," said the Inspector. He glanced round at the five children. They were horrified at seeing Goon show the false clues to Inspector Jenks. A very small twinkle came into the Inspector's eyes.

"Well, Goon," said the Inspector, "you are much to be congratulated on discovering so many clues. Er – I suppose you children haven't discovered any too?"

Fatty pulled out the envelope in which he had put duplicates of the same things that Goon had found. He undid

89

the envelope solemnly and slowly. Bets wanted to giggle, but she didn't dare to.

"I don't know if you'd call these clues, sir," said Fatty. "Probably not. We don't think they are, sir, either."

To Goon's open-mouthed astonishment Fatty proceeded to take from the envelope complete duplicates of the clues that Goon had taken out of his own envelope.

"What's all this? There's something funny about all this," said Goon faintly.

"It is certainly peculiar, to say the least of it," said the Inspector. "I am sure you children all agree with me?"

The children said nothing. They really did not know what to say. Even Fatty said nothing, though in his heart he applauded Inspector Jenks very loudly for guessing everything and giving away nothing!"

"Well," said Inspector Jenks, "suppose you replace all these various clues in their envelopes. I hardly feel they are going to help us a great deal, but perhaps you think otherwise, Goon?"

"No, sir," said poor Goon, his face purple with rage, astonishment, and shock. To think that his wonderful clues were the same as the children's – whatever did it mean? Poor Goon! The meaning did eventually dawn on him, but not until he was in bed that night. Then he could do nothing about it; for he knew he would never dare to reopen the matter of his clues again, with Inspector Jenks on the children's side.

"And now, Goon," said the Inspector, in a businesslike tone, "I propose that we go to this boy Luke and tell him to come out of his hiding-place and face up to things. We can't have him hiding away for weeks."

Mr. Goon's mouth fell open for the third or fourth time that afternoon. Find Luke? Go to his hiding-place? What in the world did the Inspector know about all that? He gave the children a glare. Interfering busybodies! Now, with the Inspector at his elbow he wouldn't even be able to scare the life out of that boy Luke when he found him, as he would dearly like to do.

"Just as you say, sir," he said to the Inspector, and rose ponderously from the ground.

"Come along," said Inspector Jenks to the children. "We'll go and have a word – a kind word – with poor old hunted Luke."

A Great Surprise

The Inspector led the way over the field and up the lane. Fatty tried to hold a cheerful conversation with Mr. Goon, but the policeman only scowled at him behind Inspector Jenks' broad back.

"In here," said Pip, when they reached his gate. They went up the drive and into the garden. Then Pip stopped and looked at the Inspector.

"Should I just go up and explain to Luke that you say he's to come out and go back to his job?" he said. "You can't think how scared he is."

"I think that's a good idea," said Inspector Jenks, "but I think the one to see him and talk to him should be me. Now, don't you worry. I know how to treat boys like Luke."

Inspector Jenks went with Pip up the garden to the summer-house. But Luke was not there.

"Oh, there he is, look," said Pip, pointing to where Luke was busy hoeing the kitchen-garden. "He says he just can't sit and do nothing, Inspector, and he thinks if he does a bit of weeding for us, it is a small way of returning a kindness."

"A nice thought, if I may say so," murmured the Inspector, watching Luke at his work, taking in the boy from head to foot. He turned to Pip.

"Just give him a call, tell him I'm a friend, and then leave us, please," he said.

"Hey, Luke!" yelled Pip. "I've brought a good friend of ours to see you. Come and talk to him."

Luke turned – and saw the big Inspector in his blue uniform. He went white, and seemed as if he was rooted to the ground.

"I didn't steal no cat," he said at last, staring at the Inspector.

"Well, suppose you tell me all about it," said Inspector Jenks. "We'll go and sit in the summer-house."

He took Luke firmly by the arm and led him to the summer-house where the children had so often talked over the mystery of Dark Queen's disappearance. Luke was trembling. Pip gave him a comforting grin, and then ran back down the garden to the others.

The children all wondered how Luke was getting on with the Inspector. They seemed to be a very long time together. But at last footsteps were heard coming down the gravel path.

All the children looked to see if Luke was with the Inspector.

He was, and he looked quite cheerful too! The Inspector was smiling his usual twinkling smile. Bets ran to him.

"Is Luke going to come out of hiding? What is he going to do?"

"Well, I am pleased to say that Luke agrees with me that it would be better to go back to his job than to hide here any longer," said the Inspector.

"But what about his unkind stepfather?" said Daisy, who couldn't bear the thought of Luke being beaten any more.

"Ah!" said the Inspector, "I must arrange about that. I had meant to have a word with him myself – but the time is getting on." He looked at his watch. "Hm, yes, I must be getting back. Goon, you must go down to Luke's stepfather at once, and inform him that the boy is not to be ill-treated. You must also go to Mr. Tupping, who, I understand, is the gardener next door, and inform him that Luke is to be taken back, with Lady Candling's permission, and is to be given a chance in the garden again."

Mr. Goon looked very taken aback. After encouraging both the boy's stepfather and Mr. Tupping to treat the boy sternly and hardly, it was scarcely a pleasant job for him to do. Fatty looked sharply at the Inspector.

"I bet he's making Goon do that to punish him for frightening a young boy," thought Fatty. Inspector Jenks fastened his eyes on Mr. Goon.

"You have understood my orders, Goon?" he said in a voice that sounded quite pleasant and yet had a very hard note in it. Mr. Goon nodded hastily.

"Yes, sir, perfectly, sir," he said. "I'll go to the boy's stepfather now, sir. Name of Brown. And I'll make it my business to see Mr. Tupping too, sir."

"Naturally, if any complaints are made to me of ill-treatment, I shall hold you responsible, Goon," said Inspector Jenks. "But I imagine you will impress it carefully on these two men that the orders are mine, and that one of your duties is to see that my orders are carefully carried out. I am sure you agree with me in this, Goon?"

"Oh yes, sir, of course, sir," said Mr. Goon. "And – er – about the stolen cat, sir. About the case, I mean. Are we to drop the case, sir – not make any more inquiries, I mean."

"Well, you might study those clues of yours and see if they shed any light on the case," said the Inspector gravely, with a wicked twinkle in his eye.

Mr. Goon did not answer. The Inspector turned to the children, and gravely shook hands with them all.

"It's been splendid to see the Five Find-Outers – and Dog – again," he said. "Good-bye – and thanks for a wonderful tea – the nicest I've had for weeks, if I may say so."

The Inspector got out his shiny black car. He roared

down the drive, waving to the children. He was gone.

"I'm going to see Mr. Tupping," said Mr. Goon, with a scowl at the children and Luke. "But don't you think this case is all closed and forgotten. It isn't. I'm still working on it, even if the Inspector don't pay much attention to it. And I'll get the thief all right in the end – you see if I don't!"

He gave Luke such a nasty look that the boy knew quite well he was still suspected. He watched Mr. Goon go down the drive on his way to see Tupping.

The children crowded round him. "Luke, did you like our Inspector? Luke, what did he say to you? Tell us everything!"

"He was mighty nice," said Luke. "Not a bit like that Mr. Goon – all threats and shouts. But how did I ever come to promise I would go back to my job – and go back to live with my stepfather, too? I wish I hadn't promised that. I'm frit."

This was a new word to the children. Bets stared at Luke.

"What's 'frit'?" she asked.

"He means he's frightened," said Fatty. "What a lovely word – frit! I shall always say that now. Frit!"

"I'm often frit," said Bets. "I was frit the other night when I had a bad dream. I was frit today when old Clear-Orf stopped to speak to us."

"And poor Luke is frit, too," said Daisy, looking at the big boy, with his untidy hair hanging over his brown forehead. "What are we to do about it?"

"If only we could find that cat," said Pip.

There came a sound from the bushes nearby. Buster pricked up his ears, gave a loud bark and flung himself into the bushes. There was a terrific scrimmage, and then something leapt wildly up a tree. The children went to see what the matter was.

They all had a tremendous surprise. Staring down at them from the tree was a beautiful Siamese cat! But it was

Luke who gave them the biggest surprise of all.

"It's Dark Queen!" he shouted. "Can't you see the ring of creamy hairs in her tail? I tell you, it's Dark Queen come back! Oh, what a queer thing!"

All the children at once saw the ring of light hairs in Dark Queen's swinging tail. The lovely Siamese swung it to and fro in anger as she watched Buster jumping up and down below.

"Take Buster away, Fatty," said Larry in excitement. "He'll scare Dark Queen and she'll run away."

Buster was shut up in a shed, much to his indignation. He nearly tore the door down in his eagerness to escape. Dark Queen quietened down when Fatty led the dog away. She sat up there in the tree, purring.

"She's thin," said Daisy.

"And look how muddy she is," said Larry. "Her coat is dirty and tangled. Let's take her to Miss Harmer. What a surprise she will have!"

Luke has a Better Time

Dark Queen allowed Daisy to lift her gently down from the tree. Then the five of them made their way with Luke down the drive, and into the garden next door.

They went to the cat-house, and on the way they met Lady Candling. She cried out in surprise when she saw a cat in Daisy's arms.

"You mustn't take my cats out of their house! Did Miss Harmer let you?"

"It's Dark Queen!" said Larry. "She suddenly appeared in Pip's garden just now, Lady Candling!"

"Good gracious!" said Lady Candling, most astonished. She glanced at Dark Queen's tail and saw the little ring of light hairs that grew there. "Yes – it's my beautiful Dark

Queen. Wherever has she been? She looks thin and half-starved."

"Isn't it a pity she can't talk, then she could tell us," said Bets, stroking the purring cat. "Lady Candling, here's Luke, too. We've been hiding him, because we were sorry for him. You'll take him back, won't you?"

"Of course," said Lady Candling. "Inspector Jenks has just been telephoning to me. Well, Luke, you can certainly come back freely now, can't you – for here is Dark Queen, returned in safety!"

"We're just taking her to Miss Harmer," said Larry. "Won't she be pleased?"

"I'll come with you," said Lady Candling. "Oh, there is Miss Trimble. Miss Trimble, what do you think has happened? Dark Queen has come back!"

"Good gracious me!" said Miss Trimble, trotting up in excitement, her glasses falling off at once. "Where did she come from? Who brought her?"

The children told her, and Miss Trimble listened in surprise, putting on her glasses again.

They all went to the cat-house. Miss Harmer was there, petting one or two of the cats, for she was very fond of them. When she saw Dark Queen in Daisy's arms she was so astonished that she couldn't say a word. She held out her arms and Dark Queen, with one graceful bound, was into them. The cat snuggled up to Miss Harmer, butting her with its head, and purring deeply and loudly.

"*Well!*" said Miss Harmer in delight. "Where did *you* come from, Dark Queen? Oh, how glad I am to have you back!"

Everyone told her at once how Dark Queen had suddenly appeared. Miss Harmer took a good look at the cat.

"I think she must have escaped from whoever had her, and made her way home – for miles probably – through the fields and woods."

At that moment Mr. Tupping came into sight with Mr. Goon. The policeman had evidently been telling him about the Inspector and his orders, and Tupping's voice was very sour. He gave Luke a scowl, and then saw Dark Queen.

Mr. Tupping seemed as if he could not believe his eyes. He kept looking at Dark Queen in amazement, and he twisted her tail round to make sure she had the little ring of creamy hairs there. As for Goon, his mouth fell open, and his eyes bulged more than ever.

His notebook came out, and the policeman began to write slowly in it. "Have to make a report of this here re-appearance to the Inspector," he said importantly. "I'd like some details. Were you here, Lady Candling, when the cat returned?"

Once more the children retold the story of Dark Queen's re-appearance, and Goon wrote busily in his black note-book. Tupping was the only person who showed no signs at all of being pleased about the cat coming back. He glared at the cat as if it had thoroughly displeased him.

"Oh, Tupping, before you go, I want to say that In-spector Jenks and I have had a talk about Luke," said Lady Candling in her low, clear voice. "And he is to start work here again tomorrow. Those are my wishes as, no doubt, Mr. Goon too has told you. I hope that I shall have no fault to find with your treatment of Luke."

Lady Candling walked off, and Miss Trimble followed her.

"Now, you clear orf," said Mr. Goon.

The children clambered over the wall and dropped down to the other side. Fatty went to let a very angry Buster out of the shed.

Then Bets' bed-time bell rang. The little girl gave a groan. "Oh, blow! That bell always rings just when I don't want it to. Haven't we had an exciting time today?"

"Well, we still don't know who did steal Dark Queen," said Larry. "I wonder if she *could* have escaped by her-self, somehow – and Luke didn't notice that she slipped off. Maybe the cage-door wasn't locked, and she pushed it open – or something like that."

"I don't think that's at all possible," said Fatty. "But we may as well think that. Anyway, we've been a failure at solving the mystery, so we'll pretend there wasn't one!

Luke went back to his stepfather that night. He was not beaten, nor was he grumbled at.

The next morning he went back to his work. He still felt very much afraid of Mr. Tupping, but that gentleman did not go for him as he usually did. Plainly, what the Inspector said had to be taken notice of! Lady Candling's orders could not lightly be disobeyed either.

The children climbed over the wall to see him as he worked.

"Hallo, Luke," said Bets. "Is it nice to be back at work?"

Luke nodded. "It is that," he said. "I'm not one for lazing around. Well, I never thanked you children properly for hiding me and feeding me like you did; but you know I'm grateful, though I can't talk easily, like you do."

"That's all right, Luke," said Larry. "We were glad to help you."

"I'll make you all whistles, if you like," said Luke. "Fine ones. Not tiddley little ones like I made for Bets. Proper big ones, and I'll paint them up for you, see?"

"Oh, thanks very much," said Pip, pleased. "I think your whistles are lovely. You will be busy if you make us each one!"

Luke *was* busy, and very happy too. Sometimes Lady Candling gave him a kind word, and the children were always ready to talk to him, or go out with him when he was off-duty.

Things went on very peacefully and happily. The days slipped by.

"It seems quite a time ago now since we thought we had another mystery to solve," said Fatty one day. "We were silly to think it was a mystery, I suppose – just a cat that disappeared, and we didn't know how. There was probably quite a simple explanation of it really."

"All the same, I wish we *could* solve a mystery these hols," said Bets. "It's not much good being a Find-Outer if you don't find out something. I wish something else would happen."

"Things never do, when you wish them to," said Fatty wisely.

But for once he was wrong. Something did happen, something that made the Five Find-Outers sit up and take notice at once. Dark Queen disappeared all over again!

The Second Disappearance

It was Luke who told the children. He came over the wall about half-past five in the afternoon, looking so white and scared that the children thought he must have had a beating from Tupping or something.

"What's the matter?" said Daisy.

"Dark Queen's gone again," said Luke. "Yes; and gone under my very nose too, just like the last time!"

"Whatever do you mean?" said Fatty, surprised. "Sit down. Tell us properly. This is extraordinary."

"Well," said Luke, sitting down on the grass beside the children, "just listen to this. I was rolling the paths round and about the cat-house this afternoon, and whilst I was doing that someone stole Dark Queen. And I never saw no one!"

"How do you know she's gone?" said Larry.

"Well, Miss Harmer had the day off," said Luke. "She went at ten, and she came back about ten minutes ago. And as soon as she went into the cage she gave a squeal, and said Dark Queen wasn't there!"

"Gracious!" said everyone. "Did you look and see too, Luke?"

"That I did," said Luke. "But there were only the other cats. No Dark Queen."

"How do you know she went whilst you were at work on the paths nearby?" said Fatty. "She might have gone before."

"No, she didn't," said Luke. "You see, Lady Candling always visits the cages now, just before three o'clock, and she and Miss Harmer talk about the cats together. Well, Lady Candling saw the cats as usual at three o'clock, and Dark Queen was there.

"Tupping took her ladyship to the cats today. He always does when Miss Harmer is out now, and she gives him any orders to pass on to Miss Harmer. I was there when Lady Candling and Tupping were looking at the cats, and I heard Tupping say, 'There's Dark Queen at the back, your ladyship – you can see the light hairs in her tail.' So she was there, then, at three o'clock."

"And do you mean to say that since three o'clock you have been near the cages, and never left them – till Miss Harmer came back just now and found Dark Queen gone?" said Larry. Luke nodded.

"And you know what's going to be said," he muttered. "I'll be accused again. I was the only one there last time, and I was the only one there this time. But I didn't touch Dark Queen."

"How did Miss Harmer find out that Dark Queen was gone?" asked Fatty, who was taking a very close interest in all that Luke said.

"Well, she came back, and Tupping met her and said he thought one of the cats wasn't very well," said Luke. "So, under my very eyes, he went into the cage, whilst Miss Harmer was coming along, and got the cat he said wasn't well, and then Miss Harmer joined him, and almost at once squealed out that Dark Queen was gone."

"Could Tupping have let her loose just in that moment?" asked Larry.

"No," said Luke. "I couldn't see Tupping in the cage,

but I could see the door quite well, and nothing came out. In fact, it was shut tight."

Everyone was silent. It did seem a most extraordinary thing that Dark Queen should have gone again, under Luke's very nose.

"Was it your own idea to roll the paths near the cat-house?" asked Fatty.

"Oh no," said Luke. "I don't do things on my own. Tupping gives me his orders every day. And he told me to spend the afternoon rolling the paths there."

"Last time you were on the spot all the time," said Pip. "And this time you were too. And last time Miss Harmer was out for the day. And this time she was too. And last time it was Tupping who went into the cage with the cats, and this time it was too – when it was found that Dark Queen had disappeared, I mean. Last time he went in with Goon – this time he went in with Miss Harmer. There are a lot of things exactly the same. It's all very, very odd."

"Well, I didn't take the cat last time, and I didn't this time either," said Luke. "I know I didn't."

"This is more of a mystery than ever," said Fatty, and he got up. "I'm off over the wall to snoop round a bit. Do you remember what we found in the cage last time? One of Luke's whistles. Well, as everything seems to be more or less the same this time, I bet there'll be one of Luke's whistles there again!"

"Don't be silly!" said Daisy. "It's just an accident that some of the things are the same."

"All right," said Fatty. "But look here, if I *do* find one of Luke's whistles in the cage, we've got to realize that *that* won't be an accident. That will be put there on purpose! Well – I'll go and see."

Everyone wanted to come, of course. So they all clambered over the wall, Luke too. Only Buster was left on the wrong side of the wall, tied up to a tree.

The five children came to the cat-house. No one was there. Tupping and Miss Harmer had gone to report the matter to Lady Candling. Only the cats looked at the children, their blue eyes gleaming. Bets counted them. There were seven.

"Look," said Fatty, pointing into the cage. "One of Luke's whistles again!"

Luke stared at it in amazement. Then he went to feel in his coat, which was hanging on a tree nearby.

"It must have been taken from my pocket," he said. "I had it in there, ready to finish. It was for Pip. And someone must have taken it."

"And put it on the floor of the cage so that you'd be suspected again!" said Fatty grimly. He stared at the whistle on the floor.

"Can't we get it out again," said Daisy. "Like we did last time?"

"I don't expect there would be time," said Fatty. "Look around for some other clues – quick."

The children began to hunt around. Bets put her nose to the cage and sniffed hard.

"There's the same smell as I smelt last time," she said.

Fatty pressed his nose to the wire and sniffed. "Yes, it's turps," he said, puzzled. "Golly! this is very queer. Everything seems to be repeating itself, doesn't it – the whistle on the floor – the smell of turps. I do think this is the strangest mystery I've ever come across."

"Fatty, I suppose this isn't a clue, is it?" said Daisy, pointing to a little round blob of paint on a stone beside the path. Fatty looked at it.

"Shouldn't think so," he said. He picked up the stone and looked at the blob of paint.

"Luke paints our whistles," he said. "Probably this is a drop of paint he spilt. Have you ever painted our whistles here, Luke?"

"No, never," said Luke at once. "I always do them in the shed where the pots of paint are kept. Anyway, I don't use that light-brown colour. I always use bright colours – red and blue and green."

"It can't be a clue," said Fatty. But he put the stone into his pocket in case.

Just then there came the sound of footsteps, and down the path came Lady Candling, Miss Trimble, Tupping, and Miss Harmer. Tupping looked important. The others looked upset, and Miss Trimble could not keep her glasses on for more than two seconds at a time.

They all looked into the cage, apparently in the vain hope that Dark Queen might possibly be there after all. Miss Harmer gave a squeal.

"What's the matter?" said Lady Candling. Miss Harmer pointed to the floor of the cage.

"What's that?" she said. They all looked in.

"Ho!" said Tupping in a ferocious voice. "That's one of them whistles Luke is always making, that is! I'd just like to know how *that* got there!"

Miss Harmer took the key of the cat-cage and opened the door. Tupping picked up the whistle. He showed it to Lady Candling.

"Is this one of the whistles you make, Luke?" asked Lady Candling.

Luke nodded. He looked very pale. He could not understand how Dark Queen could have gone again, nor how his whistle could have been found in the cage.

"Luke has been making whistles for all of us," said Fatty. He pulled his own out from his pocket. "I expect it's one of our whistles, Lady Candling."

"But how could it have got into the cage?" said Lady Candling, puzzled.

"Your ladyship, it's quite plain," said Tupping. "That boy went in to take the cat, like he did before – and he dropped this whistle by accident and never saw it. He went out of the cage, locked it, put the key back in its place, and went off with Dark Queen."

"I don't even know where the key's kept now," said Luke.

"I usually have it in my pocket, except on the days when

103

I go out," said Miss Harmer. "Then I give the key to Tupping. What do you do with it, Tupping?"

"I keep it in *my* pocket, too," said Tupping. "But I left my coat along here somewhere this afternoon, so Luke could easily have got at the key. Mark my words, Dark Queen is hidden somewhere about, ready for somebody to fetch away! I knew you'd be sorry, Madam, if you took that boy back again. Stands to reason something of this sort will happen if you do that. I said many a time to Mr. Goon –"

"I am not interested in what you say to Mr. Goon," said Lady Candling. "I think we will go over Mr. Goon's head this time and get in touch with Inspector Jenks immediately."

The children were simply delighted to hear this; but, alas, the good Inspector was away, so Mr. Goon had to be notified, and arrived, full of importance, to look for clues and to hear what everyone had to say.

He looked suspiciously at the five children. Then he looked at the cages as if he expected to find a whole lot of clues there again. But there was nothing to see except the whistle which Lady Candling had given him.

"You found any clues this time?" said Clear-Orf to Fatty.

"We've only found a smell and a stone with paint on it," said Bets. The others frowned at her so suddenly and severely that she nearly ran away.

"A smell?" said Mr. Goon disbelievingly. "And a stone with paint on? Ho! so you think you can trick me again, do you – with smells and stones this time!"

With that Mr. Goon turned his back on the children, who at once went to the wall, climbed over it, and sat down to talk about this new happening.

"Bets! Of all the IDIOTS!" said Pip. "You deserve to be spanked. Fancy telling Clear-Orf our own clues! Are you quite mad?"

"I must be," said Bets, almost in tears. "I can't think why I said it."

"Never mind, Bets," said Fatty comfortingly. "Just *because* you told him, he won't believe you – so if they *are* clues, it won't matter. Cheer up! "

"It really is a most extraordinary mystery," said Daisy.

Buster really has got Brains

"What is the most puzzling thing of all," said Fatty, "is the fact that nearly everything is the same as last time."

"It looks as if all those things had to be like that before the cat could be stolen," said Daisy.

"It's no good suspecting anyone but Luke this time," said Larry. "The cat was there at three o'clock, because both Tupping and Lady Candling saw it; and Luke was by the cat-house from three until Miss Harmer returned, and then she and Tupping go into the cage and find Dark Queen missing."

"And Luke says, as he said last time, that no one went near the cage except himself, all that time," said Pip. "Well, I simply do *not* see how Dark Queen could have been stolen."

Everyone was silent. Again it seemed an absolutely mystifying problem with no solution at all – except that Luke was a very stupid and untruthful thief. But not one of the children could believe that.

The children stayed talking until it was Bets' bed-time. Then they said good-bye and got up to go home.

"Meet here again tomorrow," said Fatty in a gloomy voice. "Not that we can do much. We'll all think hard in bed tonight and see if we can possibly find some way out of this problem."

Nobody had got any good idea when they met the next

morning – except Bets. And she hardly liked to mention her idea, because she thought the others would laugh at it.

"Anyone got anything to say?" asked Fatty.

"Well," said Bets, "I did get a sort of an idea about one of our clues."

"What?" said Fatty.

"You know that smell we smelt – turpentine," said Bets. "It was in the cage this time, and last time too. It must *mean* something – it must belong to the mystery somehow, mustn't it? So it must be a real clue, and we ought to follow it up."

"How?" said Pip, rather scornfully.

"Well, we could go and hunt about next door to find where the bottle of turps is kept or something like that," said Bets. "I don't say it will help; but after all, if it's a clue, we might find out something."

"Bets is right," said Fatty. "She really is. We did smell turps both times – and of course we ought to go and look to see if we can find where it's kept. Who knows, we might fine other clues then!"

"Let's go now, then," said Pip. "No time like the present! Come on. Look out for Tupping though. He won't like us snooping about."

They all went over the wall again, leaving poor Buster in the shed. They sent Pip into the garden to see whereabouts Tupping was.

Pip came back and reported that he was tying up something near the house. "So we're safe for a bit," he said. "Come on. Let's sniff in the cage again, and see if the smell is still there. Then we'll go hunting for the stuff."

They all sniffed in the cage. The faint smell of turps still hung there. Miss Harmer came up as the children were sniffing. She did not seem very pleased to see them.

"I don't want anyone near the cat-house now," she said. "This disappearing of Dark Queen twice running is getting on my nerves. I'd rather you kept away, children."

"Miss Harmer, do you use turps to clean out the cages at all?" asked Fatty.

Miss Harmer looked surprised. "Of course not," she said. "I use an ordinary disinfectant. Cats hate the smell of turpentine."

"Well, how did the smell of turps get into the cage then?" said Larry. "You sniff, Miss Harmer, and see if you can smell it."

But Miss Harmer had not got a very good nose for smelling, and she did not think she could smell anything like turps in the cage.

"Didn't you yesterday when you went in and found Dark Queen was gone?" said Larry.

"Well, perhaps I did," said Miss Harmer, trying to remember. "But I couldn't swear to it. I was so upset at Dark Queen disappearing again."

The children peered into the cage, still sniffing. Miss Harmer sent them off. "Do go," she said. "I really feel nervous now when anyone comes near the cats."

"Let's go to the shed and see if we can find any turps there," said Fatty. So they left the cat-house and went off to the two sheds that leaned back to back, not far from the greenhouses.

"You girls take one shed and search it and we boys will take the other," said Fatty.

So they all began to hunt hard in the two sheds, but there was no turps to be found anywhere.

Larry saw Luke passing by, looking very gloomy indeed. He whistled to him.

"Hie, Luke! You look as if you had lost a shilling and found sixpence. Cheer up!"

"You wouldn't feel very cheerful if you felt as frit as I do," said poor Luke.

"What you doing in them sheds?" he said. "You'll catch it if Mr. Tupping comes along and sees you messing about there."

"We're looking for the turpentine," said Fatty, poking

his round face out of the shed. Luke looked astonished.

"Turps?" he said. "What do you want turps for? It's kept in the other shed – on the shelf – I'll show you. But what do you want it for?"

Luke led the boys into the other shed, where Daisy and Bets were. He pointed to a shelf on which various bottles and tins stood. "It's there somewhere," he said.

The children looked. They picked up one bottle after another and sniffed it. But there was no turpentine at all.

"We've already looked, anyway," said Daisy.

Luke was puzzled. "It *was* there," he said. "I saw it myself yesterday. Where's it gone?"

Fatty began to feel excited, though he didn't quite know why.

"We've got to find that bottle," he said.

"Why?" asked Daisy.

"Don't know," said Fatty. "But we've got to. It's gone. Maybe it's been hidden away. We've got to find it."

"I bet old Buster could find it for us," said Fatty.

Luke went off to his work, still looking extremely gloomy. The others went to the wall. Pip and Fatty climbed over it and dropped down to the other side. Pip went to the garden-shed at the top of the garden, and found a small jar of turps.

Fatty opened the bicycle shed and let out Buster, who tore round and round him, barking as if he had not seen Fatty for at least five years.

"Come on, Buster," said Fatty, picking him up. "You've got to do a little work."

In a short time Fatty, Buster, and Pip were over the wall with the others.

"The coast is all clear at the moment," said Larry.

Fatty shook some turps on to his rather grubby hanky, and held it to Buster's nose. "Smell that, old fellow. Smell it good and hard. That's turps. Now, you just run all over the place and see if you can find the same smell again. Good old bloodhound, aren't you?"

Buster did not like the smell of the turps at all. He looked away from the hanky with a face showing intense disgust. Then he sneezed violently three times.

"Go on, Buster dog, find it, find it!" said Fatty, flapping the hanky at him. Buster looked up at Fatty. He knew quite well what "find it" meant. He was always finding things for Fatty. He trotted off, his pink tongue hanging out, his tail in the air.

"He's looking for rabbits, not turps," said Larry in disgust. "Look – he's found a rabbit-hole – and now we shan't be able to make him see sense for ages!"

Buster *had* found a hole. It was in a bank. He stuck his nose into it, gave a whine, and began to dig hard in his usual way, sending the earth flying out behind him.

"Come out, idiot," said Fatty. "I didn't say rabbits, I said turps."

Fatty pulled Buster out by his hind legs. Something rolled out behind the little dog. All the children stared at it. It was a cork. Fatty picked it up and smelt it.

"It smells of turps!" he said in excitement, and the others crowded round to smell it. It did. There was no doubt about it at all.

In a trice Fatty was down on his hands and knees, feeling in the hole.

He pulled out a bottle. On it was an old label, half-torn, but the letters "turp" could still be faintly seen. There was still a little turpentine in the bottle, too.

"Here's what were were looking for," said Fatty triumphantly. He showed the bottle to the others. Bets went to the hole and peered in out of curiosity.

"There's something else, Fatty," she cried in excitement, and put in her hand. She pulled out a tin. The others crowded round again to look, feeling very thrilled.

"What is it?" said Larry eagerly. "A tin of paint. Here's a knife. Let me prise off the lid."

He did so – and the children saw that the tin was nearly full of a light-brown paint.

109

"How queer!" said Fatty. "It's the colour of that blob of paint on the stone we found. Look!"

He compared the stone with the paint in the tin. It exactly matched.

"Now," said Fatty, in glee, looking at the turps and the tin of paint, "*now* – who put the paint and turps down that hole – and WHY?"

A Hunt for a Smell!

The children were terribly excited. They had two really big clues, though quite how to fit them to the stolen cat they didn't know.

"What is turps used for?" asked Bets.

"Oh, to clean paint-brushes – to get paint-marks off things," said Larry. "It's quite clear that this paint and the turps are connected in some way."

Buster had stuffed his blunt nose into the hole, and a shower of earth covered everyone. The little dog at last came out backwards, and in his mouth he held a small paint-brush!

"Listen, there's Tupping yelling to Luke," said Fatty. "We'd better get over the wall, quick. Here, Larry, just help me to clear up round this hole. We don't want whoever hid these things to see that we've found them. It would warn him – or her – that we were after them."

The boys cleared up the mess quickly, whilst the two girls ran for the wall, and Daisy helped Bets over. Then the others came, with Buster. They got over just in time, for Tupping came along that way half a minute later, grumbling away to himself.

The children retired to their old summer-house with their Clues, and looked at them closely.

"One small bottle of turps, one small tin of light-brown

paint, and one small, very old paint-brush," said Fatty. "And if we only knew how they had been used, why they had been used, and who had used them, we should have solved the unsolvable Mystery of the Disappearing Cat!"

"Fatty," said Bets earnestly, "do you think it would be any good going into the cage and sniffing about to see exactly what place had got the turps on it? I mean – if it was the benches, or the floor, or the ceiling, or the wire-netting I can't see how it would help us even if we *did* find the place that smelt of turps, but it just might."

"Seems rather a silly idea to me," said Pip.

"Well, I can't say I can see what good that would do," said Larry. "And anyway, how could we get into the cage? Miss Harmer has the key."

"Well, you know – I think there *is* something in Bets' idea," said Fatty. "Like Larry, I can't see how it would help us if we found out the exact place where the turps had been used, but I've a sort of hunch we'd better go and try. Bets, you're a good one at ideas just now."

Bets was thrilled. She did love a word of praise, because she got plenty of teasing, and praise from Fatty made up for a lot.

"Well, how could we get the key?" said Daisy. "Miss Harmer keeps it in her pocket."

Fatty thought hard for a while. "It's a very hot day," he said. "I should think Miss Harmer will have taken her coat off and hung it up somewhere. She won't be doing the cats just now – I expect she'll be at work in the greenhouses. It's part of her job to help there too, you know."

"I guess she'll have her coat under her eye, with all these disappearing acts going on," said Larry.

"Let's go and see," said Pip, getting up. He moved the loose board at the back of the summer-house and tucked the three clues there. He put the loose board over them. "There! No one will find those clues but us. Come on, let's go and see what Miss Harmer is doing.

They all went over the wall again, having first shut Buster into the shed. They couldn't have him rushing round the cat-house if they were going inside.

Fatty went to scout about and find out where Miss Harmer was. She was, as he had guessed, in one of the greenhouses tying up peach-tree branches. Fatty looked about for her coat.

It was hung on a nail inside the greenhouse where she was working. Blow! No one could possibly look for a key in the pockets without being seen by Miss Harmer! Fatty went back to the others and told them.

"We must get Miss Harmer out of the greenhouse for a minute, somehow," said Pip. They all thought hard, and some very complicated plans were talked of. It was Daisy who thought of a very simple one that could be done without anyone being seen at all.

"*I* know!" she said. "I'll slip along to the end of the greenhouse farthest from the coat – there are doors each end, aren't there? I'll hide in a thick bush in one of the beds, and then I'll call loudly, 'Miss Harmer! Miss Harmer!' And I bet Miss Harmer will walk out of the door of the greenhouse to see who's calling her, and that will just give one of you time to slip in at the other door and get the key!"

"We'd get into an awful row if anyone saw us taking the key," said Larry. "But after all, we *are* the Find-Outers, and we've got to take a few risks in our work, haven't we? Who's going to get the key?"

"I will," said Pip. "Let me do it. I'm very nippy."

"Yes, you are," said Fatty. "All right, you do it, Pip. Are you and Larry and Bets going to wait for me by the cat-house?"

"Yes," said Fatty. "Come on, let's get going, or Miss Harmer will put on her coat again!"

Daisy and Pip left the others and crept through the bushes to the greenhouses. Miss Harmer was still at work near the other end. Daisy settled herself in a thick bush near the farther end. She waited until she saw that Pip was safely in another bush near the door inside which Miss Harmer's coat was hanging.

Then the whole plan worked as if it had been oiled! "Miss Harmer! MISS HARMER!" called Daisy.

Miss Harmer heard. She turned her head and listened. Daisy called again, "MISS HARMER!"

Miss Harmer opened the greenhouse door and stepped out. "Who's calling me?" she cried. And at that very moment Miss Trimble appeared, trotting down the path, her glasses set crooked on her nose.

"Oh, Miss Trimble! Did you call me? What did you want me for?" asked Miss Harmer.

"No, I didn't call you," said Miss Trimble, her glasses falling off. "But I certainly heard someone shouting for you. Would it be Lady Candling?"

"Why does she want me?" said Miss Harmer, going up the path. "Where is she?"

"She's over by the lawn," said Miss Trimble. "I'll show you."

The two went up the path together and were soon out of sight of the greenhouse. Pip at once saw his chance, slipped in at the other door, went to Miss Harmer's coat and ran his hand quickly through the big pockets. He found the key at once!

Then he and Daisy made their way joyfully through the bushes to the cat-house, where the others were waiting most impatiently for them. "Here's the key," said Pip proudly. "Now, come on, let's hurry up and sniff round the cage."

"I'll go in with Bets," said Fatty. "Not you others, or the cats will have a fit. I've got a very good nose for smelling, and as it was Bets' idea I think she ought to come in too."

So the two of them went in together, shutting the door carefully behind them. Then they began to sniff round the cage. It smelt of disinfectant. But there was still a distinct smell of turps somewhere.

"Here, Bets, sniff just there – don't you think there's a smell of turps there?"

A big cat was lying on the bench. Bets pushed her gently away so that she could smell. "No," said the little girl. "*I* can't smell turps on this bench, Fatty."

Fatty sniffed again and looked astonished. "The smell isn't there now," he said. "But it was, a minute ago!"

Bets lifted back the cat she had moved. "There, Puss," she said, "take your place again."

"Golly! the smell's come back," said Fatty, wrinkling up his nose. "Smell, Bets."

"Why!" said Bets in surprise, "it can't be on the bench. It must be on the cat. *I* can smell it now I've put the cat back. But I couldn't before."

"Bets," said Fatty, "where do *you* smell the turps on the cat?"

"Just here," said Bets, and she bent her small nose down to the middle of the cat's dark tail.

"So do I," said Fatty. He looked very carefully indeed at the long tail, which the cat was now trying to swing from side to side.

"Fatty! Bets! There's someone coming!" cried Larry in a low voice. "Come out, quick!"

But, alas for Fatty and Bets, Mr. Tupping appeared on the scene before they could get out of the cage! And *then* there was a storm!

Mr. Tupping stared as if he could not believe his eyes. Fatty and Bets got out of the cage and shut the door, turning the key in the lock. Bets was trembling. Fatty did not feel at all comfortable himself. The other children had disappeared into the friendly shelter of the bushes.

"What you doing in there?" demanded Tupping. "How did you get the key? I believe it's you children that have been tinkering about with them cats, making them disappear! Ho! yes, that's what it is! You're the thieves, you are! I'm going straight off to Mr. Goon to tell him

114

about you – then you'll be in a pretty pickle I can tell you. And serve you right too!"

Solving the Mystery

Mr. Tupping went off, and his face was not pleasant to see. Bets was terrified. She clutched Fatty, and her face turned very pale. Fatty himself looked a bit shaken.

In silence the five got over the wall and made their way to the summer-house.

"Golly! That was a bit of bad luck," said Larry.

"We'll have to tell Inspector Jenks about it: how we took the key, and how you and Fatty sniffed all round the cat-house. Then he won't believe old Clear-Orf if he puts in a report to say he and Tupping suspect *us* of taking Dark Queen!"

Fatty was very silent. The others looked at him.

"Are you frit too, Fatty?" said Daisy. It was not like Fatty to be shaken for long. Fatty shook his head and looked very thoughtful.

"Let's think about the smell of turps on that cat's tail." he said.

"You said turps was used to get paint-brushes clean, or to get smears of paint off anything," said Bets, drying her eyes. "Do you suppose the cat had got against some wet paint or something, and the paint was cleaned off with turps?"

Fatty stared at her. Then he leapt to his feet with a yell, and smacked the summer-house table hard with his hand. His face went very red.

"What's up?" said Larry in alarm. "Have you sat on a wasp or something?"

"Listen," said Fatty, sitting down again, looking terribly excited. "Young Bets has got hold of the right idea.

115

Turps *was* used to get paint off that cat's tail. And how did the paint get there, and what colour was it? Well, we know the colour, because we've got the tin of paint that was used, and we've got a stone with a blob of that same paint on it – it was creamy-brown."

The others stared at him. Fatty got the tin out from behind the loose board and opened it. He dipped the brush into the tin and then dabbed it on the dark-brown summer-house table.

"Look at that," he said. "See that creamy patch? Well, that's what must have been on the cat's tail – in the middle of it – creamy-brown paint! And now, I ask you, what other cat has a patch of creamy-brown hairs on her tail?"

"Dark Queen!" said everyone at once. Eyes gleamed, and faces grew red with excitement as the five children worked out all that the turps and the paint meant.

"Yes," said Fatty. "And that cat whose tail smelt of turps must have had a ring of hairs in her dark tail painted a light colour, so that she might be mistaken for Dark Queen, and then the paint on her tail was rubbed off with strong turps – that's why the cage smelt of turps both times. It was done both times."

"Golly!" said Larry. "This is frightfully exciting. Somebody made a very clever plan. Let me see! I suppose Dark Queen was stolen away in the morning, and the other cat's tail painted to make her seem as if she was Dark Queen – everyone knew Dark Queen had a ring of paler hairs in her tail where she had been bitten."

"Yes; and then people came and had a look at the cats – like your mother did, Pip, with Lady Candling – and they thought the painted cat was Dark Queen; and then later on Tupping managed to get into the cage and wipe off the paint before anyone noticed it, and said Dark Queen was gone!"

"*Tupping!*" said Bets, her eyes getting large and round. "*Tupping*, did you say? But if Tupping took *off* the paint

– then Tupping must have put it *on* – and he must have been the one who stole Dark Queen, and –"

"Yes. It was Tupping. It simply must have been," said Fatty, almost beside himself with excitement. "Would you believe it? And he put the blame on Luke all the time."

"And made old Luke work besides the cages the whole time the painted cat was there till the time when he wiped off the paint and said Dark Queen was gone!" said Pip. "So that it seemed as if no one but Luke could possibly have stolen her! What a clever plan."

"Then, when he heard Bets tell Clear-Orf we had got clues of a smell and a smear of paint, he got the wind up and hid them both," said Fatty. "Afraid of finger-prints on them or something, perhaps. And old Buster found them."

"Let's get it all quite clear," said Daisy. "Tupping wants to steal Dark Queen and put the blame on Luke. He waits till Miss Harmer is out for the day – because, I suppose, he guesses she knows each cat so well that she wouldn't be deceived by painted hairs in a tail – she'd know it wasn't Dark Queen."

"Yes; so he waits till she's out, and then he steals Dark Queen, hands her over to someone, goes back to the cage, paints the other cat's tail to make it seem like Dark Queen's, sees that somebody has a look at the cats and says that Dark Queen is there – like Lady Candling did at four o'clock the first time, with your mother, Pip; and Lady Candling again, with Tupping, the second time, at three o'clock." Fatty paused and Larry went on.

"Yes; and the first time he's very, very clever. He brings back the village policeman himself to see the cats, manages to rub off the paint with a turpy rag, and then announces to Clear-Orf that Dark Queen is stolen! I must say Tupping is very cunning," said Larry. "What a nerve he must have, taking the bobby himself into the cage after he'd stolen the cat that morning."

"He managed to trick Miss Harmer herself nicely, too,

the second time," said Pip. "You remember he slipped into the cage when she came back that second time, and he must have again rubbed off the paint, and then said Dark Queen was gone. That's how it was he managed to deceive everyone. They all thought, including Luke, that Dark Queen was there all the time Luke was beside the cage – but she wasn't. She had gone in the morning. So no wonder it was difficult to clear Luke of blame."

"I suppose Dark Queen must have escaped from whoever had her, and wandered back, that first time," said Daisy. "I wonder where she is now."

"Let's telephone to Inspector Jenks again," said Pip. "Now that we have solved the mystery we ought to let him know."

"What about the key of the cat-house?" said Larry. "Oughtn't we to put that back in Miss Harmer's pocket?"

"Yes. We'll go and do that now," said Fatty.

The five children and Buster went over the wall. They hunted about for Miss Harmer but could not see her. "Perhaps she's in one of the sheds," said Fatty. They went towards a shed near the greenhouses, one they had not been into before. Fatty put his head inside.

"Hallo!" he said, "this is where Tupping keeps his things. Look! there are his rubber boots and his mack."

"What a smell of turps again," said Bets, sniffing.

"You're right," said Fatty, and he sniffed too.

The boy suddenly pulled a dirty handkerchief out of the old mack hanging up. It was marked with Tupping's name, and smelt strongly of turps.

"He soaked this hanky with turps and used it to rub off the paint he had put on that cat's tail!" said Fatty. "Another clue! Let me see! It had been raining, hadn't it, the night before, and that morning too – so Tupping would have been wearing a mack – and rubber boots too. I say, look there!"

The children looked, and there, splashed on the toes of the rubber boots, were drops of the creamy-brown paint!

Tupping must have worn the boots when he painted the cat's tail! And it was he, of course, who must have dropped a blob of paint on to the stone that Fatty had in his pocket. Probably off the paint-brush.

"We'll take these boots, and the hanky too," said Fatty importantly. "Come on, Buster. We've got some mighty good clues and bits of evidence, I must say. What a shock dear Mr. Tupping is going to get when he hears all we have to say."

They went out of the shed and came face to face with Luke, who still looked very gloomy. "You're going to get into trouble," he said to Fatty. "Tupping's gone down to get Goon, because he says he found you in the cat-house, and he says it must have been you children who took that cat. I suppose he's going to make out that you did it when I was there, and I didn't let on, so as to shield you. You're going to get into trouble!"

The End of it All

Fatty went off to telephone to Inspector Jenks. He was lucky enough to get him straight away.

"Please, Inspector Jenks," said Fatty, "we've solved the Mystery of the Disappearing Cat. Could you possibly come over and let us tell you?"

"Well," said the Inspector, "I've just had a most mysterious message from Goon — something about finding you children in the cat-house, and saying he thought you had something to do with the disappearance of the cat — and I was thinking of coming over anyway."

"Oh, good!" said Fatty joyfully. "Are you coming to Lady Candling's?"

"Yes, that would be best," said the Inspector. "Meet me there in an hour's time, will you?"

Fatty went back to tell the others – to find them all in a state of great indignation. Mr. Goon had been to Bet's mother and complained to her that the little girl had been caught trespassing in the cat-house. He had now gone to tell Fatty's mother that Fatty had been caught there too.

"Mummy is frightfully cross with me," said Bets, with tear-stained eyes. "You weren't here, Fatty, so I didn't like to say anything in case I gave away something you didn't want me to give away. So I said nothing at all, and Mummy scolded me dreadfully."

"Never mind, Bets," said Fatty. "The Inspector will soon be here, and once he hears our story he will soon put things right. We've got to meet him at Lady Candling's in an hour's time. We must take all our clues with us."

So carrying one bottle of turps, one tin of paint, one old paint-brush, one stone smeared with paint, one hanky smelling of turps, and one pair of rubber boots spotted with paint, the children set off down Pip's drive and up Lady Candling's drive in an hour's time.

"The only clue we *couldn't* bring was the smell on the cat's tail," said Bets. "And that was really the most important clue of all."

"And it was you who smelt it," said Fatty. "I must say I think you've been a very good Find-Outer this time, little Bets."

"Look! there's Mr. Goon going into the house," said Daisy. "And that's Tupping with him. And here comes Luke. Hallo, Luke! Where are you going?"

"Been told to wash myself and go up to the house," said Luke, who looked both gloomy and scared.

"Are you frit?" asked Fatty.

"Yes, I'm frit," said Luke.

"Well don't be," said Fatty. "Everything is going to be all right. You'll see. Cheer up."

But Luke could not cheer up. He walked off to wash and clean himself, looking very downcast, just as the Inspector's black car drove smartly up the drive and came to a stop. The big Inspector got out and smiled at the children. He beckoned to them.

"Who's the guilty person?" he said.

"Tupping," said Fatty with a grin. "I bet you guessed it, Inspector, though you didn't have any clues or anything."

"Well, I didn't think it was Luke, and I did think Mr. Tupping was the type," said the Inspector. "Also I happened to know what neither you nor Mr. Goon knew, that he has been mixed up in a thieving case before – dogs, it was, as far as I remember. Well, you go on in. I'm just coming."

Everyone was gathered together in Lady Candling's big drawing-room.

"Sit down, children," said Lady Candling. Fatty had left outside the door some of their clues, feeling that it would not do to let Tupping see his rubber boots, the tin of paint, or the bottle of turps. The boy did not want the surly gardener put on his guard if he could help it. The children sat down, and Fatty took Buster on his knee to stop him from sniffing round Mr. Goon's ankles.

The Inspector came in and shook hands with Lady Candling. He smiled at the children, and nodded to Mr. Goon.

"I think we'd better all sit down," he said. Everyone sat down. Mr. Goon looked important and stern. He gave Bets and Fatty a severe glance. Aha! those interfering children were going to get into Very Serious Trouble now! Tupping had reported to him that they had actually taken the key and been found inside the cat-house.

"Well, Goon," said the Inspector, "I got a rather mysterious message from you this morning – sufficiently serious for me to think of coming over."

"Yes, sir. It *is* serious, sir," said Mr. Goon, swelling up with importance. "I have reason to believe, sir, that these here interfering children know more about the disappearance of that valuable cat than we think. I think, sir, they're in for Very Serious Trouble, and a good warning from you will do them a World of Good."

"Well, I think it *is* quite possible that these children do know more about this mystery than you think, Goon," said Inspector Jenks. "We'll ask them, shall we?"

He turned to Fatty. "Perhaps you, Frederick Trotteville would like to say a few words?"

There was nothing that Fatty wanted more. He swelled up almost as importantly as Goon had done.

"I should like to say, Inspector, that we Five Find-Outers know who stole Dark Queen," said Fatty, very loudly and clearly. Tupping gave one of his snorts, and so did Goon. Luke looked thoroughly scared. Miss Trimble's glasses fell off, much to Bets' delight.

"Go on, Frederick," said the Inspector.

"I should like to explain, sir, exactly how the theft was committed," said Fatty. The others looked at him admiringly. Fatty always knew the right words to use.

"We should like to hear you, if I may so," said the Inspector gravely, with a little twinkle in his eyes.

"Well, Inspector, Dark Queen was stolen twice, as you know," said Fatty. "Both times Miss Harmer was out, and Mr. Tupping was in charge of the cats.

Mr. Goon's mouth fell open, and he stared at Fatty in astonishment.

"Now that . . ." he began – but Inspector Jenks stopped him.

"Don't interrupt, Goon," he said. And old Clear-Orf dared say no more.

"I'll tell you how it was all done," said Fatty, enjoying himself immensely. "The thief stole Dark Queen out of the cage in the morning; but he cleverly painted a ring of hairs a creamy colour in another cat's tail, so that to anyone not knowing the cats extremely well that other cat seemed to be Dark Queen!"

There was a chorus of exclamations. Miss Trimble's glasses fell off immediately.

"Well," went on Fatty, "you can see that anyone coming to see the cats in the afternoon would think Dark Queen was there – but she wasn't. Then, when the right moment came, the thief hopped into the cage, rubbed the paint off the cat's tail with a rag soaked in turps, and then announced that Dark Queen was missing! So, of course everyone thought the cat must have been stolen in the afternoon, whereas she had been taken in the morning."

"And that's why everyone thought it was *me* that took the cat," broke in Luke. "Because I was the only one near the cage in the afternoons, and no one came near but me."

"Yes," said Fatty. "That was part of the plan, Luke. The blame was to be put on to you."

"Who was it?" demanded Luke, his face going scarlet with rage. "Just let me get my hands on him, that's all!"

The Inspector sent a glance at Luke and the boy sat back saying no more.

"How do you know all this?" asked Mr. Goon, his face a mixture of amazement, disbelief, and scorn. "It's just a silly make-up. You got to have proof of these things before you can say them."

"We *have* got proof," said Fatty triumphantly. He put his hand into his pocket. "Look! here is the bottle of turps. It was hidden down a rabbit-hole, with a tin of light-brown paint, used for the cat's tail, and an old paint-brush. Larry, get the other things. They're outside the door."

Fatty brandished the bottle of turps and the paint-brush for everyone to see. Miss Trimble's glasses fell off again, and she was too nervous to replace them. She stared at the clues with short-sighted eyes, and looked at Fatty as if he was the greatest detective in the world.

Larry brought in the rubber boots and the tin of paint. He set them down before Fatty. Tupping's eyes nearly fell out of his head when he saw his own boots there.

"Now," said Fatty, picking up the tin of paint, "here's the paint that was used."

"These boots were worn by the thief," said Fatty, and

123

he pointed to the drops of light-brown paint on them. "And this is the handkerchief he soaked with turps, and used to wipe off the paint as quickly as possible from the cat's tail when he went into the cage – first time with Mr. Goon, second time with Miss Harmer."

"May I see that handkerchief?" said the Inspector with great interest. He took it and smelt it. The smell of turps was still very strong on it. Fatty took the stone from his pocket, the one with the smear of light-brown paint on it. He handed it to the Inspector too.

"We found that just outside the cage, sir," he said. "That was one of our clues. The other clue was the smell of turps in the cat-house. Little Bets spotted that. She was a splendid Find-Outer."

Bets went red with joy. The Inspector beamed at her. He looked again at the handkerchief.

"This handkerchief has someone's name on it," he said. "I imagine it is the name of the thief?"

Fatty nodded. Luke leaned forward.

"Who is it?" he said. "Go on! you tell me who it is."

"Yes, whoever is it?" said Miss Harmer.

The Inspector looked gravely round the little company. Tupping had gone pale, and he kept swallowing hard. All his insolence and conceit had gone. One by one the others looked at Tupping and knew who was the thief.

"Tupping, what have you to say about all this?" said the Inspector in a voice gone hard as iron.

"What, it's *Tupping*!" said Mr. Goon in a half-choked voice, and he glared at the gardener with hatred and scorn. "*You!* Sucking up to me: taking me into the cage with you; telling me a pack of lies and making me look foolish like this!"

"Well, Bets told you we had two clues, a smell and a stone with paint on," said Fatty. "And you only laughed."

"Tupping, where is the cat?" said the Inspector, still in the same hard voice. "You understand that there is no possibility of the charge made against you being false.

There are other things, in your past, which fit in very well with this."

Tupping crumpled up completely. From a harsh, cruel, bad-tempered man he turned into a weeping coward, and it was not a pleasant sight.

"Bullies are always cowards," Fatty whispered to Larry.

Suddenly Tupping began to pour out a confession. Yes, he had stolen Dark Queen. He had owed money to someone, and he had thought of taking the cat. He'd tell who had got it and the police could get it back. He *had* tried to put the blame on Luke. He *had* painted the other cat's tail, and he *had* used turps to get off the paint quickly. He'd done it twice, because the first time the cat had escaped and come back. He was sorry now. He'd never do a thing like that again.

"You certainly won't, for some time at least," said Inspector Jenks grimly. "You will be in a safe place, out of harm's way, and I don't think anyone will be sorry. Goon, take him away."

Goon put a heavy hand on Tupping's shoulder and jerked him to his feet. He looked with great scorn at his prisoner.

"You come-alonga-me," he said in a fierce tone. The Inspector spoke to Goon in an icy voice.

"You do not seem to have shone at all in this case, Goon," he said. "You appear to have made enemies of those who were on the right track, and to have actually made friends with the thief himself. I hope in future you will be a little more careful. I trust you agree with me?"

"Er – yes, sir; certainly, sir," said poor Goon, looking very woeful all of a sudden. "Did my best, sir."

"Well, very fortunately these children did better than your best, Goon," said the Inspector. "I think we can be very grateful to them for their work in solving the Mystery of the Disappearing Cat. I hope that is your opinion too, Goon?"

"Oh yes, sir," said Goon, purple in the face now. "Very clever children, sir. Pleasure to know them, sir."

"Ah! I'm glad you agree with me," said Inspector Jenks in a more amiable voice. "Now, please remove that man."

Goon removed Tupping. The children heaved a sigh of relief. "Well, he's gone!" said Daisy. "And I hope he never comes back."

"He will certainly not come back here," said Lady Candling, who had listened to everything in the greatest astonishment. "As for poor Luke, I hate to think of all he has gone through because of that wicked Tupping."

"That's all right, your Ladyship," said Luke, beaming all over his face. "If you'll keep me on, Madam, I'll work hard for you till you get a new gardener. And I'll never forget these here clever children — it fair beats me how they solved that mystery."

"It was really Bets who put us on the right track," said Fatty. "Good old Bets!"

"Oh, we all did it together," said Bets. "Buster too. Well, I *am* glad everything's turned out all right, and I expect you'll get your cat back, won't you, Lady Candling?"

"We'll see to that," said Inspector Jenks, getting up. "Well, I must go, and once more, allow me to say that I am very pleased to have had the help of the Five Find-Outers — and Dog! I trust I may have your help again in the future. I hope you agree with me?"

"Oh *yes!*" said all the Find-Outers, going out to the car with the big Inspector. "We'll let you know at once if we've got another Mystery to Solve!"

Another Mystery? Well, I expect they'll have one all right. I must tell you about that another time!"

DRAGON BOOKS

Thousands of children buy a Dragon book every week. *Why don't you?* Think of it, in no time what a wonderful library you would have, all of your very own. How gay those Dragon books on your bedroom shelf, favourites to read and re-read again and again. Ask your mum or dad if you can order a Dragon book every week from your bookseller or newsagent. After all, it's only 12½p. If you have difficulty in getting titles, they are obtainable from: Cash Sales Dept., P.O. Box 11, Falmouth, Cornwall, at the price shown plus 4p postage.

All at 12½p (unless shown)

Green Dragons
Pony Books

By Mary O'Hara

My Friend Flicka Part 1	Thunderhead Part 3
My Friend Flicka Part 2	Green Grass of Wyoming Part 1
Thunderhead Part 1	Green Grass of Wyoming Part 2
Thunderhead Part 2	Green Grass of Wyoming Part 3

The above are all books about Flicka in order of appearance

By Gillian Baxter

Jump to the Stars	Tan and Tarmac
The Difficult Summer	Horses in the Glen
The Perfect Horse	Ribbons and Rings

By Christine Pullein-Thompson

The First Rosette 17½p	The Empty Field 17½p
The Second Mount 17½p	The Open Gate 17½p
Three to Ride	The Pony Dopers

By Elyne Mitchell

The Silver Brumby 17½p	Silver Brumbies of the South
Silver Brumby's Daughter 17½p	Silver Brumby Kingdom

Adventure Stories

By William F. Temple

Martin Magnus, Planet-Rover   17½p   Martin Magnus on Venus   17½p

By Arthur Catherall

Ten Fathoms Deep	Forgotten Submarine
Jackals of the Sea	Sea Wolves

By Showell Styles

Midshipman Quinn	The Ladder of Snow
Quinn of the Fury	A Necklace of Glaciers
The Shop in the Mountain	The Pass of Morning

By David Scott Daniell

Mission for Oliver
Polly and Oliver

Polly and Oliver Besieged

By Edgar Rice Burroughs

Tarzan of the Apes
The Return of Tarzan
The Beasts of Tarzan
Tarzan and the Ant-Men

Tarzan's Quest
The Warlord of Mars
Thuvia, Maid of Mars

The House in Cornwall
Adventure in Forgotten Valley
The Mysterious Rocket
Dolphin Island
An Edge of the Forest
Australian Adventure
The Three Musketeers

Noel Streatfeild
Glyn Frewer
André Massepain
Arthur C. Clarke
Agnes Smith
Maria Wolkowsky
Alexander Dumas

All at 17½p (unless shown)

Red Dragons

By Enid Blyton

Mystery of The Burnt Cottage
Mystery of The Disappearing Cat
Mystery of The Secret Room
Mystery of The Hidden House
Mystery of The Spiteful Letters
Mystery of The Pantomime Cat
Mystery of The Missing Necklace
Mystery of The Invisible Thief
Mystery of The Vanished Prince
Mystery of The Strange Bundle
Mystery of Holly Lane
Mystery of The Strange Messages
Mystery of Tally-ho Cottage

First Term at Malory Towers
Second Form at Malory Towers
Third Year at Malory Towers
Upper Fourth at Malory Towers
In The Fifth at Malory Towers
Last Term at Malory Towers
The O'Sullivan Twins
The Twins at St. Clare's
Summer Term at St. Clare's
Second Form at St. Clare's
Claudine at St. Clare's
Fifth Formers at St. Clare's
Mystery of The Missing Man

Mystery of Banshee Towers

The Coral Island   12½p
Knights of the Cardboard Castle   12½p

R. M. Ballantyne
Elisabeth Beresford

Blue Dragons

By Enid Blyton

The Red Story Book   12½p
The Blue Story Book   12½p

The Yellow Story Book   12½p
The Green Story Book   12½p

Eight O'Clock Tales   12½p